KEN

if you were with me everything would be all right

"By turns funny and moving, sweet and bracing, Ken Harvey's stories are full of the real thing— what one of his lovable characters calls 'the soft and distant thump of life.' A pleasure to read this talented debut collection."

Philip Gambone
author of *The Language We Use Up Here*

"These are gorgeous, heartfelt, mesmerizing stories. In fact, so much so that when I finished Ken Harvey's book, I was faced with a major dilemma: Should I go right out and start buying copies for my friends or turn back to the beginning and read all thirteen stories again?"

Claire Cook
author of *Ready to Fall*

"Ken Harvey, in this book of thirteen stories, presents a fascinating mix of people, people searching for love, love that unites, that enriches, that inspires, that heals, that saves. He writes with wit, tenderness and compassion."

Raymond DeCapite
author of *Go Very Highly Trippingly To and Fro*
& *The Stretch Run*

if you were with me everything would be all right

•

s t o r i e s

if you were with me everything would be all right

•

s t o r i e s

Ken Harvey

A Pleasure Boat Studio Book

Design & Composition by Shannon Gentry
Cover Photograph by Tim Hall

Library of Congress Catalog Card Number: 00-101772
Harvey, Ken
If You Were With Me Everything Would Be All Right
& Other Stories / Ken Harvey
ISBN: 1-929355-02-5

First Printing

Published by PLEASURE BOAT STUDIO
8630 Wardwell Road • Bainbridge Island • WA 98110-1589 • USA
Tel/Fax: 888.810.5308
E-mail: pleasboat@aol.com • URL: http://www.pbstudio.com

ACKNOWLEDGMENTS
A number of the stories in this collection were previously published, often in a different form: "If You Were With Me Everything Would Be All Right" and "Mariposa" (under the title "Migration Routes") in *The Evergreen Chronicles,* "So This Is Pain" in *Other Voices,* "Tipping Cows" (under the title "Cows") in *The Nebraska Review,* "33 1/3" in *The Massachusetts Review,* "Sugar Boy" in *The James White Review,* "The Last Warm Day" in *The North Atlantic Review,* "Just Looking" in *The Baltimore Review,* "Mr. Bubble, I Love You" in *River Styx.* "Paper Man" was published in *The Worcester Review* shortly after the release of this collection.

THANKS
Many years ago Ed Burdekin suggested I write, so I did. He has read almost every word I've written since then, and has been my steadiest supporter and dear friend. These stories simply would not have been written without him.
Jennie Rathbun is a wonderful writer, reader and friend. Writing group members Rachel Solar-Tuttle and Cindy Revelle also offered good advice.
Thanks to the Massachusetts Artists Foundation for the generous financial support.
And, of course, thanks to Bruce. This is for you.

Printed in Canada

FOR BRUCE

Contents

IF YOU WERE WITH ME EVERYTHING
WOULD BE ALL RIGHT

In the used bookstore, an old white house off the Maine Turnpike that smelled of pine shelves, Owen was looking through some postcards next to a stack of *Saturday Evening Posts*. He picked one of these cards out of the bin to study more carefully, a blue and green sketch of the Thousand Islands International Bridge between Ivy Lea, Ontario, and Colin's Landing, New York. The caption called the bridge "the largest international project in the world" since it was made up of five bridges, including the "World's Smallest International Bridge and having ten miles of highway through the very heart of the Thousand Miles."

"What's so interesting?" Arthur asked.

"These bridges, that's all," Owen said. "You know me." Owen was an architect and was fascinated by the structure of things. "What about you? What'd you find?"

"A few books. That Gielgud bio I'd been looking for," Arthur said. "It's time to pick out your print like you promised. You feeling OK now?"

Owen had gotten dizzy in the car. He said it was a little light-headedness when he asked Arthur to drive for him. They'd come up from Boston that morning to Ogunquit where they'd planned to have dinner and browse in this store that also sold maps, historical documents, and various prints: flowers, birds, and turn-of-the-century sketches of a number of Maine's colleges, including Bowdoin, where Owen had gone over twenty years ago. Arthur never missed a chance to be sentimental and wanted to buy him a print of the college for his birthday. Because Owen thought the gift too expensive, he insisted on paying for dinner this evening as well as a room the two of them were to share in the motor lodge.

In turn, Owen agreed to pick out a print of his alma mater, even though he hated reminders of his youth. Owen was about to turn forty-five, an age, he sometimes thought, when anything good that happened to him would have to be labeled "a long time coming." He was slowly losing the lovely reddish brown waves of hair that made him so attractive all his life, and now wore glasses more to hide the thin lines around his eyes rather than to improve his vision.

"I'm feeling better, I guess," Owen said to Arthur now. He ran his finger along the International Bridge on the card, picking up dust. It seemed odd talking about his own health since Owen was used to worrying about Arthur and when he would eventually get sick. At first he thought he could handle that Arthur was infected, but as the two of them considered shifting their lives for each other, perhaps even living together someday soon, Owen had begun to panic.

Owen put his hand on top of Arthur's, the first time he

had touched him since their argument in the car. It had started when Arthur suggested a word game, a simple one, he explained. All you had to do was name a topic, like gay bars, Sundays, sex, pets. The other person then tells what he either loves or hates about the subject. You could take your pick.

"You start," Arthur had said. He took a sip of coffee from the Styrofoam cup in the rack between the two seats.

"Me?" Owen said. "But it's your game." It was so like Arthur to start something, then throw the responsibility to someone else. Sometimes Arthur would call at night, say hello, then wait for Owen to pick up the conversation. Arthur was younger than Owen by about ten years, but that shouldn't mean Owen always had to take the lead.

Owen switched lanes quickly, making Arthur spill some coffee on his chest.

"Shit. My new T-shirt." Arthur directed a gay theater company in Boston and in the summer wore T-shirts from what he called his gay musical collection. Today he had on a shirt with two men dancing in farmer's overalls and straw hats with the title "Oklahomo!" at the top.

"You can soak it at the motel," Owen said.

"Well?" Arthur asked. "Are you going to play or not?"

"I really don't know how to begin," Owen said. He looked at his odometer to see how far it was to Ogunquit. The numbers seemed blurred. Then, when he squinted, he imagined the numbers were years in the future spinning by. He suddenly wondered how much longer Arthur would be with him.

"Just start," Arthur said.

"How do you get points?"

"This is just a game to know each other better. It's not a competition."

"OK, OK," Owen said. "Let's see. How about love?" He was hoping he might catch Arthur off guard and win this game, even if Arthur didn't want to give out points.

"I don't know," Arthur said. "There's so much. You know, like falling in love or being in love or falling out of love."

"You said just name one thing."

"Fine," Arthur said. "I'm going to surprise you. I'm going to tell you something I *hate* about falling in love. What I really hate is that all those fucking Dionne Warwick songs actually start to make some sense. That drives me crazy more than anything." He flipped his bare feet up on the dashboard and folded his knees under his chin.

"Arthur, that's ridiculous."

"What do you mean? I think my answer sort of covers it all," Arthur said. "Have you really listened to the lyrics to one of her songs? They're insanely trite and weepy and make total sense once you're in the throes of romance."

"'You'll Never Get To Heaven If You Break My Heart,'" Owen said. "Yes, my dear. That about covers it all."

"Look, I didn't say I *liked* the songs. I didn't even say that they moved me. I just said that I understand them."

"Actually, I think they do move you, Arthur," Owen said with a smirk. "That's what scares me."

"Fuck you."

"Now wait a minute," Owen said. "I was only kidding. I like how sentimental you are. It's kind of cute."

"I said fuck you."

"Come on. This was supposed to be fun, remember? We were going to smooth things over."

A few nights earlier they'd had a "crisis," as Owen called them. Arthur had arrived to pick him up for the movies. Owen was changing his clothes.

"Owen," Arthur began. "I need to ask you something."

Owen took off his shirt and rolled some deodorant under his arms. "What is it?"

"I don't know. It's hard to explain. I just get the feeling you don't like touching me anymore. I mean, we hardly ever hug just to hug and when we make love, it's like you're not really with me."

"Arthur—"

"No, listen to me. Please," Arthur said. "Why don't we ever talk about living together anymore? For a while we were checking the papers all the time for a place. That all sort of fizzled out. Is it because you don't want to sleep with me every night?" Arthur waited for an answer but Owen turned his back to get a fresh pair of socks out of his bureau. "I guess I feel like you're trying to reposition me in your life. Are you?"

Owen pulled off his jeans and stuck his hand in his bikini briefs to adjust himself. "The only thing I'm trying to reposition right now is in my shorts."

"Don't ignore me," Arthur said. "Why can't you even deal with my hands on you anymore?"

"Don't take things so personally," Owen said. "It's like the doctor slapped you on the ass when you were born and you've taken everything to heart ever since."

"I'm not going to let you shove me aside without talking about it," Arthur said. "Come on. Tell me. Tell me you're bored or angry or afraid I'm going to infect you or *whatever*. Just tell me what's going on."

"I don't want to have this conversation," Owen said. Arthur's eyes started to well up as they often did when he and Owen fought. He bit his lower lip and blinked his eyes quickly.

"Look, I'm sorry," Owen said. "I just get nervous, that's all. It's me. I guess I'm scared." He touched Arthur's hand.

Now, in the bookstore, Owen touched Arthur's hand again.

"I'm sorry about the misunderstanding in the car," Owen said. "Forgive me?"

"Sure," Arthur said.

The two of them were quiet. Finally Arthur took the postcard of the Thousand Islands International Bridge from Owen's hand to fill in the void. He turned the card over.

"Did you read this?" Arthur asked.

On the back of the card was a two-cent Canadian stamp and the postmark June 7, 11:00 P.M., 1938, Brockville, Ontario. There was writing in black ink that varied light and dark depending on the angle of the fountain pen. The card was addressed to Robt. Carrington, 29 Childs St., East McKeesport, Penn., USA. It read:

> Bob:
> If you were with me everything
> would be all right.
>> Stanley

*T*hey had dinner in an old inn that was a five-minute walk from the motel. Arthur said he was hungry and ordered a chicken dish with a rich white sauce. He stuffed himself with buttered rolls before the meal. The doctor had told him it was a good idea to gain a few pounds.

Owen was beginning to feel light-headed again, and he didn't know why. He was the healthy one of the two, with no trace of the virus to worry about, and he ran about six miles a day. At the motel he had gotten so dizzy in the shower that he had to hold onto the towel bar so as not to slip. Steam rose in a dense hot cloud around him, and Owen had the sensation that if he fell he might drop miles and miles before hitting the ground. He felt he was being pulled, although he had no idea where.

"It's very clear to me," Arthur said. He swished the wine in his glass to make a little whirlpool. "Bob and Stanley were lovers—if not in a totally sexual way at least *emotionally*, and I believe they at least kissed, if not more. Then Stanley got scared of his passion and fled. My guess is that Stanley got married quickly and went on his honeymoon with— let's say her name is Suzy—and then, once there with his wife, got this intense longing for Bob and wrote him the card."

"I think you're reading way too much into it," Owen said. He took off his glasses and rubbed his eyes. "Do you really think Stanley would write something so obvious on a postcard that anyone could see? Even if there was something only remotely romantic between them, he'd never take a risk like that."

"That's part of the charm of it," Arthur said. "They were so innocent about the whole thing, so totally and obliviously in love"

"I doubt it," Owen said. He sipped the tea he'd ordered, hoping it might soothe him. "I think it's much more likely that Bob and Stanley were business partners and that Stanley was up in Canada trying to cut a deal of some sort. Somehow he blew it—or blew some part of the deal, the part Bob would have been able to pull off. So he wrote him the card."

"In that case he would have called," Arthur said. "You just don't want to see what's right in front of your eyes."

"You've been listening to too much Dionne Warwick."

"It's like you don't want to believe that two men could love each other as dearly as Bob and Stanley obviously did," Arthur said. "Christ, you sound so straight when you talk like this, like one of those tediously stuffy academics who never want to believe Willa Cather was a lesbian."

The waiter came. Owen signed the bill and put his American Express card back in his wallet. "You go back to the motel and I'll take a walk. Maybe some fresh air would do me good. I'll be in later on."

"Don't be that way," Arthur said. "Can't we even discuss something like a postcard? I just think it's funny how resistant you are to Bob and Stanley's romance, that's all. Why won't you even consider the possibility unless it's completely spelled out for you? It's like one of those buildings you design. You need a blueprint first."

*O*wen sat on a bench along the Marginal Way, a narrow dirt path of about two miles that overlooked the ocean. He watched the last flashes of sunlight trickle off the water as it got dark. Two elderly women dressed neatly in slacks and sweaters walked by arm in arm. One had long silver hair that blew off her shoulders in the wind. They smiled at Owen as they went by him. The one with the silver hair said "hello" and the other, who seemed a bit older, said something about it being such a beautiful evening. Owen must have been distracted by something—his dizziness, perhaps, or the ocean—because by the time he spoke to agree with her, to tell her it really was a gorgeous night, the two women were gone.

Owen heard a rustle in the bushes to his side. He thought it might be an animal, although he had no idea what kind of animal might live so close to the ocean and the populated business area a minute or so away. Maybe a deer or a skunk. A sharp ocean breeze cut across his face and Owen brought his hands up to rub his cheeks for warmth. He felt the salt from the water on his eyelids. He thought he might be getting dizzy again but couldn't really tell while he was sitting, so he stood up slowly, his hand on the end of the bench. He began to feel a stirring inside him, or even a cracking of something brittle, perhaps his very bones.

"You're not going anywhere before you give me my postcard back. Hand it over."

The man had come out of the brush area where Owen had heard the noise. He was about Owen's age and wore a white suit with pleated pants, a white shirt, and a thin black tie. On his lapel was a sprig of magnolia blossom that Owen assumed he'd just cut from shrubbery along the Marginal Way. When the man took off his Homburg hat, Owen noticed that his hair was slicked back.

"I'm Stanley and I said I want my postcard back. The one you bought for fifty-two cents this afternoon." He put the hat in front of Owen so he might drop the postcard inside.

Owen looked away. He slowly stood on his toes hoping he might see the two women again over the tops of the dense shrubbery.

"I'm waiting, pal," Stanley said. He tapped his foot. "And don't start moaning about how you're feeling. I know you're dizzy. That was me stirring things up a little before my grand entrance."

Owen put his hands in his pockets. "I'm afraid I don't have your postcard. I left it in the motel room. I think it's on top of the bureau."

"You *think* you know where it is? Boy, are you something." Stanley took out a Lucky Strike and lit it. "Now sit down."

Owen obeyed and Stanley sat next to him. Stanley crossed his legs and took a leisurely drag of his cigarette, blowing little rings of smoke when he exhaled.

"You smell like Old Spice," Owen said. "I hate that stuff. It reminds me of my father."

"Sorry. We didn't have Obsession to splash on like you boys do nowadays." He hit the pack of Lucky Strikes hard against the side of his hand until a cigarette popped out. "Want one?"

"No, thanks," Owen said.

"You thought we were *business* partners? Oh come on now, honey." Stanley shook his head disapprovingly. "Well, let me tell you something. I don't believe you love Arthur in the least. There. How do you think *that* feels?"

"But I do love Arthur," Owen said.

"Ohhh," Stanley said. "Now I'm supposed to believe you." Stanley put his cigarette on the edge of the bench, then took his magnolia blossom off his lapel and began plucking the petals one by one. "He loves him. He loves him not. He loves him. He loves him not." Stanley threw the stem over his shoulder. "Sorry. I don't buy it."

"How was I supposed to know you loved Bob?" Owen said. "There wasn't enough to go on."

"Wasn't enough to go on," Stanley said in mocking voice. "Well in case you have learned by now, Orson—"

"Owen. The name's Owen."

"Pardon me." Stanley sighed in exasperation and for a moment Owen was afraid he might not continue. "Now are we going sit here and play Name That Skeptic or do you want to hear what I have to say?"

"Sorry," Owen said.

Stanley was quiet. It had gotten darker and Owen had a hard time seeing him, so he reached over and touched Stanley on the knee to make sure he was still there.

"Get your hands off me," Stanley said. "What are you doing cruising some guy you only know through a post-card? And what about that sweet little Arthur who's all by himself in a motel watching Siskel and Ebert fight over their favorite Shelly Winters' movie?"

"I wasn't cruising you."

"Oh, please," Stanley said. "By the way, what did you think of her in *The Poseidon Adventure*?"

"I never saw it," Owen said. "I didn't go to movies much once I was in college."

"I never saw it either," Stanley said. "I didn't go to movies much once I was dead."

"So what were you going to tell me?" Owen said in the darkness. "You started to say something about me not having enough to go on."

"What I was going to say," Stanley said, "was that in

case you haven't learned by now, we never have that much to go on."

Owen wanted to touch him again but resisted. He brought his knee up to the bench and twisted his body so it faced Stanley. Owen could still see the outline of Stanley's long nose and could tell he'd put his hat back on. Below them, the tide had come close enough so that Owen could hear the water splashing against the rocks.

"What do you mean by that?" Owen finally asked.

"Shit," Stanley said. "I've got to be pithy, too? Isn't it enough that I've come back to talk to you? I hate it when people demand I say something meaningful. I just can't take the pressure." Owen heard Stanley take his handkerchief out of his pocket and wipe his brow.

"I don't mean to pressure you."

"It's not your fault," Stanley said. "What I'm trying to tell you, Otto—"

"Owen."

"What I'm trying to tell you, Owen, is that sometimes the only evidence you get in life is a cheap postcard of the Thousand Islands International Bridge. Now I know that's a pretty flimsy thing to pin your faith on, but love, it's about as sure a bet as you're going to get in this world." When Stanley stood up, his knees cracked. "Bob used to hate that sound. It drove him crazy." Stanley walked around the bench as if to get the kinks out of his legs.

"So why'd you leave him?" Owen asked.

"That really doesn't matter," Stanley said. "What matters right now is that you don't leave Arthur or let Arthur leave you. Understand?"

"I think I do."

"Good," Stanley said. "Now do you guys have any good plans for the summer?

"Well, Arthur made plans for us to go on a cruise."

"Really?" Stanley said. "Now that sounds a lot more romantic than that tacky motel you're in tonight." He suddenly sneezed, then sneezed three or four times again in rapid succession. "Damn allergies. Bad time of year." He blew his nose.

"We're going on the *Queen Mary*. Did you and Bob ever go on it?"

Stanley gave a little laugh. He was standing right next to the bushes where he had first appeared. "Owen, dear, you're *looking* at the Queen Mary."

Arthur was asleep in the motel. The TV was on, perched on the wall across from Arthur's feet. He had been watching the Weather Channel. A list of temperatures around the country was running down the screen against some canned elevator music. Owen turned the TV off and sat at the edge of the bed.

Arthur was naked. Owen rubbed his hand along his shoulder and down his side. He brushed his fingers against his hips and legs. "Hey," Arthur said, slowly turning to Owen. "Did you have a nice walk?"

Owen said nothing but took off his clothes. He climbed into bed and pressed himself tight against Arthur. He kissed him on the forehead and on the lips.

"Hold me," Owen said.

"Sure."

They held each other with their heads on the pillow.

Owen stroked Arthur's hair and goatee.

"You didn't tell me how your walk was," Arthur said.

Owen hesitated. He wrapped his arms as tight as he could around Arthur and let out a sigh of pleasure. "That's how my walk was," Owen said. "It was as nice as that."

"Good," Arthur said.

When Owen let him go, Arthur pushed himself up on his elbows and looked around the room as if trying to wake up by exposing his eyes to light. He got out of bed and went into the bathroom. Owen heard him pee.

"I think I'd like to go for a walk, too," Arthur said when he came back into the room. He stood at the foot of the bed.

"I came back because I wanted to be with you."

"Well, you can walk with me," Arthur said. He stretched his arms over his head and yawned.

"I really don't feel like getting dressed again," Owen said.

"Then we won't."

"Thanks. Let's just stay here and snuggle, OK?"

"I meant we won't get dressed. We can still go for our walk," Arthur said. He extended his arms to lift Owen off the bed.

"What are you talking about?"

"Nobody's going to see us. It's dark outside. Come on, Owen. Be a little daring, will you?" By now Arthur was leading Owen to the door.

"But it's chilly out there. Really. You'll catch a cold."

"I'll survive," Arthur said. He opened the door and led Owen onto a small wooden porch. The two of them ran behind the hedges that lined the Marginal Way.

"I've never done anything like this," Owen said. They

were now walking on tiptoe to avoid cutting their feet on the sharp stones sticking up in the gravel. Owen wrapped his arm around Arthur's waist, then rubbed his hand quickly along Arthur's side to keep him warm. Arthur stopped and turned to Owen. They kissed.

"Let's go down by the water," Arthur said.

Arthur led Owen by the hand down some large red rocks, waiting for him at the end of every step to make sure he didn't slip. The tide was still high when they finally reached the bottom of the hill.

"Let's put our feet in the water," Arthur said. He sat on a rock next to Owen.

"Are you crazy?" Owen said. "The water's freezing. I just wanted to look at the ocean for a minute and then go back."

Arthur didn't say anything. He lowered his legs and kicked his feet when a ripple from a wave came by. Arthur waited for Owen to follow.

"My ankles are aching," Owen said when his feet finally touched the water. "It's so fucking cold."

"You'll get used to it," Arthur said. He leaned back against the rock and opened his arms wide. Owen thought that he had never seen anyone look so free as Arthur did right then.

"Arthur," Owen began. "I think you were right about the postcard. About Stanley and Bob, I mean. I don't know why I didn't want to think they were lovers. Of course they were. I know that now."

"You were just trying to reposition them," Arthur said. He turned to Owen and touched his cheek.

Owen reached for Arthur's hand and looked up at the

stars. They were silent for a while.

"In a way it was cowardly of me not to believe they loved each other," Owen said. "I don't know why. It just feels that way to me now."

Then, to prove to Arthur that he was ready to take a leap of faith he hadn't taken with Stanley and Bob, Owen stood on the rock and walked into the ocean. He turned and saw Arthur's silhouette behind him. Owen felt a sharp pang of grief when he saw Arthur that way, dark and without features. When Arthur yelled not to worry, that he was there to save him if the tide got too much, Owen relaxed. He swam farther out. His skin tightened from cold. As he swam deeper and deeper, he grew numb until he couldn't tell his own body from the water around him. Owen stopped to let his legs rise to the surface and to stretch his arms. The surf gently lifted and lowered him. He turned his head and looked to the shore. At this distance, Arthur had completely faded from view. Owen rolled his head back and watched the sky, trying to find Arthur's face in the configuration of stars, like some new constellation. Please be with me, Owen thought. Be with me here, in this new territory of ours, where nothing seems young, not you, not love, not even death.

MR. BUBBLE, I LOVE YOU

In September of 1975, ten days after he began his new teaching job, my father was suspended for a semester when he told his ninth grade civics class that he thought communism was a damn good idea. "They asked my opinion," he said to my mother and me at the kitchen table. "I gave them an answer." Wax dripped down the candle in the Chianti bottle he was rotating and hardened on his thumb. Donovan played in the background.

"You did the right thing," my mother said, stabbing her fork into the mushroom polenta.

"There's a lesson in this for you, Ho," he said. My full name is Hopi, given to me because my mother and father were teaching on an Arizona Indian reservation when I was born.

"What lesson?" I asked.

"Speak the truth no matter what," my father said. "Don't conform as people would expect you to. Transcend your genre." His tone implied that a boy of twelve shouldn't need him to spell such lessons out.

"Your father is a man of integrity," my mother said. "He has made his beliefs clear to the school from the start."

Just that August we had moved from Hammond, Indiana. I loved that long ride across Pennsylvania and through Southern New England. My parents were always busy with one political action or another, so we didn't spend a great deal of time together. After two days we arrived in Lynn, Massachusetts, the basset hound of cities. At the Woolworth's downtown, dead goldfish floated pink and scaly in the aquarium. Nobody cared. You had to be oppressed to feel at home here.

"I feel like I've been here all my life," my mother said as she unpacked her loom from the U-Haul. "I love this place already."

"It feels like a therapist's dream," my father said.

"Not *therapist*, Landis," my mother corrected him. *"Life situations adjuster."* She said it was a more empowering title for her work. She also asked her patients to call her Violet, not Ms. Wiley.

We lived in a two-floor apartment above Dino's Pizza. My bedroom overlooked Wyoma Square: the Dairy Queen, Sozio's Magnavox Appliances, the BP Gas Station, Ryan's Chicken Pot Pies, Same Day Cleaners, and a beauty salon named Curl Up and Dye. Our new place had an eat-in kitchen, a breakfast nook, and a dining room. My mother also had her own closet for the first time, where she hung her peasant skirts, her shapeless, baggy blouses with their hand-embroidered designs, and her only dress. The dress was my favorite of all her clothes. It was deep blue, like a night sky, with brilliant quarter moons and stars all over. Purple triangles that looked like teepees ran around the hem. I loved the silky feel of the dress. I could imagine blowing away if I wore it in the wind.

My father was prematurely bald, with hair only on the sides of his head, as if somebody had started to shell an egg and stopped halfway down. He wore a goatee, too, and wire-framed glasses, making him look in his mid-forties instead of the thirty-four years he really was. On the other hand, my mother always appeared younger than her age. Her soft strawberry-blonde hair, the faint spray of freckles across her cheeks, even her slight overbite gave her an almost school-girl look. She was very pretty, more attractive than my father, and I sometimes wondered if she married him to prove that looks did not matter when it came to love.

My mother set up her Life Situations Adjuster office in a spare room off the kitchen of our apartment. She advertised in the Lynn *Daily Evening Item* and distributed flyers, and soon she had a steady stream of clients whom she often met on evenings and Saturdays to accommodate their work schedules. Sometimes they waited at our kitchen table for their appointments, eating homemade peanut butter cookies and sipping the French roast coffee my mother had brewed for them. She told me not to go into the kitchen when she was working, but often I pretended to need a napkin or a glass of water so I could sneak in and see her clients.

One skinny woman with hair like Cher's came early and sat down at the kitchen table with a slice of Dino's anchovy pizza. She got so nervous that she threw up all over her beautiful yellow sundress and white Dr. Scholl's. From then on, I thought of that woman as Lunch. Miss Drum was the teenage girl who drenched herself in cheap perfume that smelled like Janitor in a Drum. Double Dip was the black man who came to each session with a Dairy Queen dipped in cherry. But my favorite, the man I waited every Saturday afternoon at two to see in our kitchen, was the man who always smiled and smelled of soap: Mr. Bubble.

I had no idea why Mr. Bubble was seeing my mother. He was tall and young and handsome and happy. He lived in Peabody. He wore a pin-striped sports coat with white pants, beige suede shoes, and suspenders. If he'd worn a hat, you might think he was a singer in a barbershop quartet.

One afternoon I put away the peanut butter cookies and took out a package of fancy pastries someone had given my parents as a gift.

"*Petit fours?*" I offered Mr. Bubble.

"*Mais oui,*" Mr. Bubble said, putting his hardcover edition of *Sense and Sensibility* on the counter. He took the pastry between his index finger and his thumb. He ate it in three tiny bites, removed the perfectly folded handkerchief from his sports coat, and dabbed the corners of his mouth.

There was so much I loved about Mr. Bubble, not just how he ate his *petit fours* and Oreos and peanut butter cookies. I also loved how he inhaled the smell of his coffee before taking a sip. How he used a shiny, light blue ribbon as a bookmark instead of folding the page corners. How his socks always matched his tie. How his cologne blended into his own clean, soapy smell and didn't overpower you like Miss Drum's perfume did. And how he never, ever, unlike many people I knew, started singing the seven dwarfs' "Off to Work We Go" song when he greeted me. Mr. Bubble simply said, "Hi, Ho."

"Have a seat," I said, pulling out a kitchen chair. "Would you like some coffee with the pastry?"

"Oh, please."

He sat down, laced his fingers on his lap, and smiled.

"Lovely day," he said.

"Yes," I said. "Here."

Mr. Bubble picked up the earthenware cup I'd placed for him at the table while I lifted the coffee pot. I watched him close his eyes as I poured. His eyelashes were soft and blonde, like the camel hair on an artist's brush.

"Ooch!" Mr. Bubble said. He dropped his hot cup on the floor. It broke, and some of the pieces skidded under the table across the red and white linoleum.

"I'm so sorry," I said. I grabbed a dishtowel and started wiping the coffee I'd spilled on his light trousers. "I guess I wasn't paying attention."

"Here, let me," Mr. Bubble said. He took the towel from me, ran it under the faucet, then rubbed the stain.

"I feel awful," I said. "You'll never speak to me again."

"It's just a pair of pants. They can be cleaned in a day."

"I'll pay for the cleaning," I offered.

"Don't be silly, Ho," Mr. Bubble said as he joined me to pick up the pieces of the cup off the floor. "Don't cut yourself."

"Are you sure you're not angry with me?"

"Of course not."

"Would you think of coming a little early next week, just so we could have some coffee that I won't spill on you?"

"It's a date," Mr. Bubble said.

*T*he following Saturday, my father knocked on my bedroom door.

"Want to go to the Topsfield Fair?" he asked.

"I thought you were going to that no-nukes demonstration at Seabrook."

"Canceled. I've got the day free. What do you say? Just you and me. When was the last time we spent a whole afternoon together?"

What could I say? That I'd decided over the course of the week that I had fallen in love with Mr. Bubble? That I'd glued that broken earthenware cup back together and placed it on my bureau, a memento of the "yes" he'd given me when I asked him out on, to use his word, "a date?"

"When will we be back?" I asked.

"Five or six. Meet me downstairs in half an hour."

I needed to let Mr. Bubble know that I wasn't standing him up. I tore a sheet out of my French notebook and cut the curled edges so the paper looked a little more presentable for my note:

> Hello,
>
> I wish I knew your phone number so I could call you to let you know that my father is making me go to the Topsfield Fair this morning. I hope you won't be too upset with me when you arrive ahead of your scheduled appointment only to find me not there. Please let's try to meet again next week at about 1:30. For now, the petit fours are in the fridge. I'm looking forward

to seeing you next week.

Your Friend,
Ho

I rolled up the note and tied it with a pink ribbon. Then I stuck it in the repaired earthenware cup and placed it at his seat at our kitchen table.

By the time my father pulled into the parking lot of the fair, it had begun to rain, and our VW got stuck in the mud. He bought me a ticket and I passed through the turnstile to the fairgrounds, where people were huddling beneath the awnings of the cotton candy and turkey legs booths.

"No rides," my father said as he lifted his Totes umbrella up high enough for both of us. "Somebody's always paying somebody off to avoid inspection."

"But there's a Ferris Wheel."

"I'm sorry," he said. "Besides, do you know what they pay those poor men who run those things? Peanuts. We can't go supporting that."

"Then why are we here?"

"Don't be that way, Ho," my father said. "The 4-H Club does some interesting things with pumpkins."

I followed him to the pumpkin exhibit. In the center was the largest pumpkin at the fair, some 2000 pounds, but it had lost all shape of a normal pumpkin. It looked as though somebody had dropped it down from the sky. Instead of breaking into a thousand pieces, the pumpkin just sat there, like a huge orange blob of Silly Putty.

"I've got to go to the bathroom," I said, just to get out of Pumpkin Pavilion.

My father followed me to the men's room which was in the horse show building. The air reeked of soggy hay and horse dung.

"I'm going to walk around a little," my father said, "but I'll meet you right here in a few minutes."

Inside the men's room an old man sat at a table with a plate in front of him. Men dropped nickels on the plate as they left.

I found an empty stall and went in. I checked the seat cover to make sure there wasn't any pee on it, then pulled down my pants and sat. I waited for something to happen, but nothing did, so I pulled on a few pubic hairs just for the fun of it. They were still pretty new to me, and I liked hold-ing a single hair up to the light and seeing how curly it was compared to the lifeless hair on my head.

"Shhh," said a man's voice in the stall next to me.

"Don't worry."

I heard a little rustling and somebody breathing sort of heavy, like the guy had asthma. I dropped my head down below my knees to look under the stall divider. All I could see was a pair of beige work boots and the bottom of the guy's jeans. Whoever was in there was standing up, facing the toilet, like he was about to pee.

I pulled up my pants and stood on the toilet to get a look on the other side. There were two men in the stall, both I'd say in their twenties, one wearing a cowboy hat and sitting on the tank of the toilet while the other man leaned over and held him. He kissed him gently on the neck, then stifled a giggle as he took the cowboy hat off and put it on his own head. When he started kissing him again, it was on the lips this time, a long slow passionate kiss that made my neck pound hard. The man on his feet lowered the other's suspenders with a quiet snap. Then he unbuttoned the man's red flannel shirt, revealing a dark, smooth chest.

I felt dizzy, trying to keep my balance and holding my breath so the men wouldn't hear me. My legs began to shake. I reached for the divider, but I couldn't grab hold of it quickly enough to keep me steady. My arms started making wider and wider circles, like someone who was about to fall off a diving board. I landed feet first in the toilet with a splash.

"What's going on in there?" yelled the old man at the table.

"Shit," whispered one of the cowboys. I heard some scurrying; one of the men had sneaked underneath to the neighboring stall.

I climbed out of the toilet and flushed, just to sound normal, and took out a quarter to drop in the man's plate as I ran out.

Where was my father? My legs were sopping wet up to my knees, and I wanted to go home. I followed the jingling of the horses into the arena. A man dressed up in a studded black outfit was sitting in a huge wagon driving six horses around in a figure eight for the judges. He reined them to a stop and reversed direction. I looked into the stands and couldn't see my father anywhere.

Outside the arena, people were still milling about even though the rain was coming down hard. I heard some screaming and then some loud booing from the crowd just ahead of me. The sign above read "Jimbo's Pig Races" and listed the pigs who were presently racing: Piggly Wiggly,

Bacon and Legs, Hammy Davis Junior, Porky and Bess. I squeezed through the crowd to get a better look.

A man was lying in the middle of the muddy track as one of the pigs with a pink bow on its neck stuck its snout in between the man's legs, smelling him like a dog might smell a mate. I covered my face when the two cops came to remove the man from the track. It was my father.

"Ho!" he yelled.

I wanted to grab my father's umbrella and open it in front of my face so no one would know who I was.

"Ho, come here!"

I had to feel my way through the crowd since I refused to look up and see where I was going, but when I finally got to my father and the two cops, I looked right at him.

"What do you think you're doing?" I asked.

"It's inhumane to do that to our porcine friends, Ho."

"I'm humiliated," I said. "Look at you." He had mud all over his face and plastered to his goatee and hair. I gulped when the cop put the handcuffs on him.

"You'll remember this, Ho," my father said as we pulled out of the Fairgrounds in the police cruiser.

"You bet I will. The first day in decades you decide to do something with me and I lose out to Hammy Davis Junior."

"No, I mean it," he said. "You'll remember this in a good way."

"There is no good way of seeing your father arrested for messing with pigs."

"Oh, but there is," he said. "Sometimes you have to lie down to stand tall."

My father was right, of course. I did remember that day at the fair, and I remembered it in a good way, but it had nothing to do with him. I couldn't get the kissing cowboys out of my mind. I didn't say a word on the ride home, I just looked out the window and revisited again and again those two men in the stall next to me. It had never really occurred to me that men could actually kiss that way, the way I'd caught my mother and father kissing on the sofa when I'd come through late at night to get a glass of water. Or the way Ron Howard and Cindy Williams kissed in American Graffiti. Or even the delicate way some couples kissed in ads for Maxwell House coffee. But once I saw those men kiss, I reworked the scene as many ways as I possibly could: I was the one on the toilet tank, then the one standing up, then wearing a cowboy hat, then opening up my shirt, then opening the other guy's shirt. I was even in a dress once, just for the fun of it, and let the cowboy reach beneath my hem as I gasped with pleasure. And then at last, I was in that stall with Mr. Bubble. He loosened his tie as if to let out some hot air, lifted it over his head, and put it around me. We kissed.

My father finally pulled into Wyoma Square.

"I'm sorry if I embarrassed you," he said.

"I'll be all right," I said.

"But I'm not ashamed of what I did."

"I get it, Dad," I said, and started running up the stairs to see if Mr. Bubble had left me a message in the earthenware cup.

The cup was exactly where I left it, at Mr. Bubble's seat. There was a note inside, without the pink ribbon, but it was a note all the same.

To me. From Mr. Bubble.

See you next week, Ho.

*T*hat night my mother cooked Indian food, rice with cur-
ried red potatoes and pumpkin with fenugreek seeds. We
ate by the candlelight of the Chianti bottle, and listened to
some Joni Mitchell.

"So what do you think the Lynn School Board will do?"
my mother asked after my father told her about his arrest
for defending the pigs.

"My guess is that nobody will ever find out," my father
said. "Who reads the Topsfield papers?"

"That's true," my mother said.

"Not that it would change things if they did, Violet."

"Oh, I know that. It's just that it'll be nice having two
salaries again. I don't want you losing your job for good.
This living by your principles can get a little draining."

"I don't want Ho getting the wrong message," my father said. "You need to do what's right in the world."

"I had I really good day, Dad," I said.

"Really?" my father said. He ruffled my hair, but it was
like someone was giving him stage directions in an earphone.

"I did," I said. "I discovered something very important
about me and about life."

"Tell us, Ho," my mother said.

"I figured out I love men."

A fenugreek seed got stuck between my father's teeth,
and he tried to remove it with his tongue.

"That's nice," my mother said. "We should love everyone."

"Your mother's right," my father said.

"What I mean is that I love men more than I love women."

They were silent for a moment. My father reached for a toothpick to work on his seed, and my mother ate some of her pumpkin dish, followed by a long swig of Chianti.

"The pumpkin is a very neglected vegetable at the American dinner table," she said.

"I saw these two guys kissing at the fair," I said.

"We heard you, Ho," my father said.

"I guess that's fine for now, dear," my mother gulped.

"But never forget that all struggles in life are class related," my father added.

My parents didn't refer to my declaration at all that week. It was like the time I confessed to liking Elton John's music: they tolerated it because they were tolerant people and I was their son, but they didn't like it. I can't say they bothered me too much since I really couldn't think of anything else but Mr. Bubble and our date the following Saturday. I carved his initials in one of the mattress boards of my bed ('Mr. B,' inside a sorry-looking heart), imagined him stepping out of the shower before he put on his dapper clothes, and even mentioned his name in every example of my vocabulary assignment: Use the following words in original sentences that clearly reveal their meanings:

My friend Mr. Bubble **exudes** sophistication and *savoir faire*.

I didn't have to **cajole** Mr. Bubble
to be my friend.

Mr. Bubble and I do not have an
adversarial relationship.

When Saturday finally arrived, I woke up early and picked out three shirts to wear, trying each one on with and without a T-shirt, looking in the mirror, tilting my head this way and that, brushing my hair away from my forehead then letting it fall back down again for a more casual look. I chose a red-and-white-striped cotton button-down shirt, khaki pants and brushed-back hair because I thought that's what Mr. Bubble would have chosen for himself. At one o'clock, I decided to walk off some of my nervousness, so I put on my sneakers and went downstairs to Wyoma Square.

It was a beautiful day, warmer than you'd expect for mid-October, so nice that someone drove by in a old convertible with the hood down. I looked in the window of Sozio's Appliances and saw all TV's tuned into the Saturday morning bowling show, then peeked in at some of the women getting their hair done in the beauty salon. I walked to the Dairy Queen where the weather had brought more customers than usual for this time of year, then headed back to our apartment above Dino's Pizza. By the window I saw a man and a woman sharing a large pepperoni pizza and a pitcher of Coke.

What was this? I recognized the woman as one of my mother's clients and, even though the man's back was to me, I could tell right away who was in that pin-striped sports coat. Only Mr. Bubble wore a coat like that. I walked a few steps to the side just in time to see the two of them burst into hysterical laughter, then watched his gentle, pale hand fall effortlessly on top of hers. I folded my arms hard across my stomach to keep from crying. Mr. Bubble—*my* Mr. Bubble—was having lunch with Lunch.

I ran to my room and threw myself across the bed. Who could I talk to? I don't know whether or not I would have actually gone to them if they were available, but right then I was furious at my father for being at his anti-nuke meeting in New Hampshire and at my mother for sitting behind a closed door adjusting Double Dip.

I tore up the vocabulary sentences I'd written about Mr. Bubble. Anyone who laughed with Lunch didn't *exude* sophistication; maybe our relationship was a little *adversarial*; and, most of all, maybe I did have to *cajole* Mr. Bubble to be my friend. But how could I compete with Lunch?

By now it was 1:30, the time I was supposed to meet Mr. Bubble in the kitchen. I closed my eyes and took a series of deep breaths to calm down. I checked the mirror to make sure my face was no longer flushed and entered the kitchen just as Mr. Bubble was opening the door.

"Hi, Ho."

"Hello," I said. "Sit down."

"Sorry we missed each other last week," he said. "Did you have a good time at the fair?"

"It was most memorable," I said distantly.

"That's lovely."

"And I'm sorry to say I have another engagement today. I do hope you'll excuse me."

"Why, of course, Ho," Mr. Bubble said. "You have a nice day. We'll see you around."

I nodded to Mr. Bubble and returned upstairs. I went to my mother's closet and took out her blue dress with the quarter moons and stars and her dress shoes. I found the only lipstick she owned: pale pink, so you could hardly tell you had it on. I brought everything to my room.

My heart was pounding. I felt like a character in the climax of a long novel. *She dressed herself quickly in her finest dress. Her hand shaking, she applied her lipstick and wiped the excess color off her chin with a tissue. She sat on the edge of the bed, remembering the words of her father, who had died in the terrorist bombing of a plane destined for Cairo: "Sometimes you have to lie down to stand tall." She stared at the clock. She wanted the timing to be perfect.*

1:55. My mother's sessions ended at ten minutes to the hour, so Double Dip was gone by now. She usually spent the time before her next session writing notes or clearing her mind with a quick meditation. At 2:00 exactly she'd come into the kitchen to meet Mr. Bubble, then invite him into her office. That's when they would hear the commotion.

I ran downstairs to the street. I pressed the walk light, and the red and yellow appeared. Then I walked into the middle of Wyoma Square, where five streets came together from every direction, and I lay down.

Once the lights turned green, some of the drivers started to honk. I opened my eyes a crack to see two women in curlers come out of Curl Up and Dye to see what was going on. The customers at Sozio's came out too, and three or four people each holding a slice of pizza from Dino's. More and more horns were tooting and many of the drivers got out of their cars. Before long a crowd of people had gathered around me. An old woman tapped my leg with her cane to make sure I was alive.

Finally, I heard my mother scream as she broke through the crowd. Mr. Bubble was right behind her when she knelt down next to me.

"Oh, God. What's going on?" she said. "What are you doing?"

I remained silent until Mr. Bubble kneeled down opposite my mother and took my hand.

"Are you OK, Ho?" he asked.

I gave him the faintest smile, then let out a breath, as if it were my last.

"Mr. Bubble, I love you."

"**Y**ou could have gotten killed," my father said when my mother told him what happened that night. "What made you do such a thing?"

"You told me to transcend my genre," I said. "You told me to stand tall."

"Shit, Ho," my father said. "Pigs are one thing. Cars in Wyoma Square are another."

"I've given my client a referral to go somewhere else," my mother said. "But I think you need to see an adjuster of your own, Ho."

"He needs a shrink, Violet," my father said. "He's our only son, for God's sake."

"We want you to know we can handle the 'boy meets boy' part of you," my mother said. "But we draw a line at suicide, don't we, Landis?"

"I wasn't trying to kill myself," I said.

"That's for Dr. Breese to determine," my mother said.

Dr. Breese was a skinny, middle-aged woman with butterfly glasses who believed in sand therapy. She sat me down by an elevated sandbox in her office to take notes on what I built. For three weeks I drew little bubbles with my index finger. Finally Dr. Breese called my parents in for a family meeting.

"His behavior implies some underlying need," she said.

"I agree," my mother said, as if she were grading Breese on her oral exams.

"We must find out what is lacking in his life," Breese continued, looking down at her notes. She spoke in a sort of psychobabble—that only my mother seemed to grasp—about my adolescent development and the importance of consistency. Then she suggested I needed to have adults in my life who taught me more than how to peaceably protest cosmetic testing on bunnies. She looked at my father when she said this.

"I try to spend time with him," my father said.

"There is no blame here," Breese said in her most hopeful voice. "Only opportunity." She raised a fist in front of her flat chest and gave a little punch in the air as if to say *Go team!*

My father tried to follow Breese's advice, taking me to the Metro Bowl in Peabody a couple of times and buying us tickets to a few Celtics games. But he just couldn't help himself: The machines that reset the candlepins stole jobs from needy men who had restood them by hand years ago, and pro basketball exploited black athletes. Soon he was back filling his time at anti-nuke meetings, writing press releases for Amnesty International, and running for president of the

Lynn Teachers Union.

Over the next few weeks, I thought about Mr. Bubble a little less, dreamed about him a little less, and even hoped I would hear from him a little less. I stopped wearing a folded handkerchief in my shirt pocket and never finished *Sense and Sensibility*. But I still missed him. Every morning I would fill up with sadness when I smelled the soap lather in the shower. I couldn't walk by Dino's Pizza without a gulp, and I nearly burst into tears the night my mother served us *petit fours* for dessert.

On my thirteenth birthday my father pleaded guilty to disorderly conduct at the Topsfield Fair and paid a $500 fine. Early that evening, we had a special birthday dinner of spinach gnocchi and listened to Crosby, Stills, Nash and Young. My father gave me a book of Frank O'Hara's poetry and Ginsberg's *Lectures on Poetry, Politics, Consciousness*. I had my first glass of wine. It took me two tries to blow out the candles of my poppyseed cake.

"So, Son, are you happy?" my father asked.

"I've never been happier," I said, but of course I was lying.

SO THIS IS PAIN

In the Central Plaza of Oaxaca, Mexico, a boy named Pedro was trying to sell Lena his collection of brightly colored wood creatures: green fishes, yellow lizards with two heads, and, Lena's favorite, the porcupine with red-tipped quills that for a moment she imagined might shoot off the animal's back through the air. Lena knew it was a wives' tale that porcupines threw their quills, but she wasn't sure what to believe these days. Beside the boy was his younger sister, Manuela, no more than five or six years old, who doubled over now and then and complained in Spanish that her bones hurt. Pedro told Lena that if she bought just one thing he could buy his sister's medicine this week. Lena doubted the girl was sick but pulled the pocketbook over her head anyway. For a week now, Lena traveled in fear that something would be taken away from her, so to protect herself from thieves she carried her purse strapped in a tight diagonal across her heart.

Lena counted the money for the porcupine while Manuela reached out and took the hem of the *gringa's* dress between her fingers. When the wind came the girl let go, and the gingham blew enough to show off Lena's long, slender legs. In school Lena was called lanky. Her guidance counselor at Lynn English High, a bald ornithologist named Mr. Twitchell, began Lena's recommendation to Salem State College by calling her "ostrich-like," then proceeded to compare her to any number of birds that Lena had never heard of, like guillemots and grackles and todies, until he ended by saying she would someday possess the grace of a swan. Lena was accepted that March as an education major. "I am not surprised," Mr. Twitchell said, "but I do hope you know it was my reference to *Parus atricapillus*, the Black-capped Chickadee, that did it." He then handed her a gift, a book called *Winging It: An Amateur's Guide to Bird Watching.* "Congratulations," he said. "Treasure this."

By her twenties, Lena's thinness and stature had, as Mr. Twitchell predicted, developed into elegance, and by her thirties, a seductive grace that she used in her work as a bearer of bad news. She had been giving people bad news for over a year now, ever since she quit her position as a Spanish teacher at Pickering Jr. High, and was making a decent living from the business. Her company, a one-woman operation called *Don't Kill the Messenger*, was listed in the yellow pages under "Information Services." She was hired to break the news of sexual betrayal and death: An unfaithful uncle runs off with the family fortune; Oliver, Mrs. Gusterson's parakeet (*Melopsittacus undulatus*, Lena noted on page 72 of her now-beaten old book) escapes and is mauled by a cat on the Peabody line, the case Lena's husband Eliot referred to as *Oliver Twisted*.

Lena worked up to delivering four or five pieces of bad news a day. *The Lynn Daily Evening Item* did a story on her as part of a series on entrepreneurial spirit in the dying city ("Bad Tidings She'll Bring To You From Your Kin," July 16, 1996). Lena was hit with a rush of adrenaline whenever she gave her news, and she pictured all the little bronchial tubes in her lungs opening up, like the diagrams in the ads for one of those miraculous asthma mists. ("My lungs *tingled*," she later told her shrink. "Have your lungs ever tingled?") She practiced the bad news on Eliot. She sat down on the bed that they still shared, looked him in the eye and said, "Your wife recently slept with another man. She wants you to know that she really didn't enjoy it, and that by the end of the encounter she was so nervous that she peed all over the black satin seat of the rowing machine. Forgive her."

On vacation in Mexico, Lena practiced to keep from losing her touch, reporting late arrivals and cancellations to fellow passengers. Once, to a striking mustachioed man at the Mexico City airport, she mentioned the possibility of a crash, a small one, with only the minor parts of the plane breaking off. She practiced with Pedro and Manuela, too, in the Oaxacan square. "You poor girl," she said in Spanish. "You have that look about you my husband had right before he died." This was not true. Eliot was not dead and Lena did not believe the girl was sick, but everything was a lie of sorts when you spoke a language that wasn't your own. Lena turned to Pedro. "Pray for your sister," she said. Manuela looked at Pedro in a panic. Lena motioned to the enormous cathedral behind them that cast a shadow across the plaza as dusk set in. "Go in there and pray."

A small brass band of old men was seated in folding chairs at the edge of the plaza. The men began to play a slow melancholy song while lovers walked arm in arm past the cathedral. Vendors sold cigarettes and cups of roasted corn.

"Go," Lena whispered to the brother and sister.

*T*he sign on Lena's hotel room wall read "Rules and Regulations for the Visitor." Among the list of rules were fire instructions, check-in and check-out times, and a warning in English that "anyone who creates a scandal or performs immoralities will be axed to leave." It took Lena a moment to figure out that by "axed" they really meant "asked," and she was relieved that her body wouldn't be taken out of the room in green garbage bags if anyone should happen to catch her touching herself in the shower.

Axed to leave. Lena put down the porcupine she'd bought and ran her finger under the misspelling to make sure she was reading correctly. This morning in the English section of the book store she'd read *The Lives of Myrna Loy* for *The Lives of Mayan Lords*. She wondered if she'd gotten lazy in her thirties or if she was subconsciously filling in words she really wished were in front of her. Her shrink, this heavy, white-haired woman who Lena felt knew nothing, told her this misreading was a metaphor for the changes happening around her. "Your *perspective* on life is evolving. Your husband is not the only one who is changing," she said. She was frumpish and Lena wondered what she looked like having sex.

"Why don't you ever call me by my name?" Lena asked.

"I do have a name, you know. Why don't you use it? I came here to find out who I am, Dr.—"

"Fleece."

"Right. I knew that, Dr. *Fleece*." Lena repeated the name too clearly, as if teaching the vowel sounds in one of her language classes. She went on to say she felt her life was like one of those bad TV movies where everything is based on a real story, but you never know how much is true.

"Now why do you give out these pieces of bad news?" Dr. Fleece asked.

"Because I don't want to open fire in a crowded McDonald's," Lena said. She twirled her hair around her finger.

"Yes," Dr. Fleece said. She lifted a glass bowl off the floor. "Peppermint?"

"*L*et's break rule number six," Lena told Alessandro, a young Italian tourist with long sideburns Lena remembered from the seventies. She'd met him in the square, not far from where she bought the porcupine when she first arrived a week or so ago. She spoke slowly to Alessandro, in a mixture of English and Spanish, a little of each he understood. Rule number six was the ax rule. Lena stretched out next to Alessandro on the bed. The hotel room had soft pink walls with molding made of dark wood. The windows had no screens, just metal bars to keep out the pigeons (*Zinaida aurita*, page 63) but not bugs, and mosquitoes buzzed around the ceiling light. Lena watched them swirl as Alessandro ran his finger along the inside of her leg. She wondered if Eliot would consider this cheating, or whether or not she should.

"What do you do for work, Lena?" Alessandro asked.

"I used to be a teacher," she said. "*Profesora*."

"Ah!" Alessandro said. A sly smile crossed his face. "Can you teach me something?" He opened his eyes wide and laughed at the joke that seemed more clever than it was.

Lena lowered the straps of her dress off her shoulders, then pulled the top of the dress down to her waist. Alessandro leaned forward, ready to kiss.

"First, just look," Lena said. Alessandro stared at her breasts, then reached out. Lena finally let him touch.

Lena took Alessandro's wire sunglasses out of his shirt pocket before she unbuttoned him and rubbed her hand across his chest. She gently pressed her index finger against his nipple and he did the same to her. Once Lena was hired by a woman to tell her husband she planned to have her breasts reduced. Lena sat with him in a fast food roast beef sandwich shop near Lynn Beach and broke the news to him while he was eating french fries. His wife told Lena he'd be there, so Lena walked in and found him, the short balding man with a red mustache, just as she described. Lena asked to join him. "By this time next week," Lena said as if reading a fortune cookie, "your wife will have smaller breasts." The man choked on his fry.

"Do you like my breasts?" Lena asked Alessandro.

Alessandro responded by taking one in his mouth.

"Are you jealous?" Lena asked. "*Celoso*?"

Alessandro stopped and looked up.

"Of my breasts," Lena said. "Do you want them?"

Alessandro laughed. Lena took his head and lowered him back towards her.

At first Lena's husband was jealous, but he never used that word. "I envy you," he said one night when Lena came out of the shower. She went with him and he touched her all over, innocently, like a child examining his own body for the first time. Lena spread out on the bed while he caressed her. Eliot was tall and broad-shouldered with large, soft hands. He gently opened her legs when he kissed her, a reverential peck of a kiss like the kisses the priests at St. Pius gave the Bible during mass. "Lena, I want these things," Eliot said.

"What things?"

"These." Eliot cupped her breasts. "And down here, too."

Lena tried to believe Eliot was setting her up to make love. She put her fingers on the buckle of his jeans. "You have them."

"No," he said. "I mean really. I want them to be mine."

Lena took her hands away from his pants. "What are you talking about?"

"Bert Parks," Eliot said.

"What?"

"Miss America, 1967, the year Miss Massachusetts, a girl from Saugus, came in first runner-up. She did 'Over the Rainbow' in pantomime. My mother wept when she flapped her hands to the 'happy little bluebirds' part. I was twelve. When they got to the swimsuit competition I thought I should be getting a hard-on but instead I was feeling like I wanted to look just like one of those girls walking down the runway. I watched Bert Parks size all the contestants up. I pictured myself up there and wondered what he'd think of me if I had a woman's body. I really wanted him to like me. I tore his picture off the cover of a magazine and taped it to my mirror. Whenever I got dressed I pretended he was watching me, singing that Miss America song over and over again." Eliot was crying now. When he ran his hand through his blond hair, Lena noticed his roots had begun to turn gray.

Eliot pulled the sheet out from the mattress to wipe his nose and eyes. Lena took a pillow and held it across her.

"Why do I feel I should be more surprised about this?" Lena said. "Jesus."

"You pick up things."

"Those *Playboy* magazines I found under the cushion of your chair that day," Lena said. "I knew there was something wrong with them. I mean, the pages weren't even wrinkled. Not a smudge. You weren't even jerking off. I might have been hurt if you were, but I could have understood that."

"For me they were like those coffee table books with huge travel pictures in glossy color. My mother used to keep one of the English countryside next to her bed. It's where her parents came from, but she'd never been there. She used to open the book before she went to bed and look at the photographs. 'Someday,' she said. 'Someday I'm going to get there. It's where I belong.'" Eliot wrung his hands. "Life's been sort of like that travel book for me, too."

"But we're not dealing with a little field trip here. What the fuck are you going to do about this?"

Eliot told Lena about hormones that would help his breasts grow and make him lose some body hair. That would take a while. Then there was an operation at some gender identity clinic.

"You mean they're going to cut it off?"

"I don't see it as losing something, Lena."

"Jesus Christ. I want to hit you. I'm sorry, Eliot, but I really want to hit you while you're still a man." Lena got up from the bed and threw on a dress. She wondered how much like her Eliot wanted to look. Maybe he'd even tried on her clothes when she wasn't around.

"Believe it or not, I still love you, Lena."

"Sure. Right. That certainly straightens things out."

"We don't have to end, Lena. We can move out west somewhere and buy a new place, live like sisters. We can grow a garden."

"A garden? You want me to fucking plant bulbs with you?" Lena walked to the door. "Tell me one thing, Eliot. Where does it go once they cut it off? Can they give it to a girl who wants to go the other way? Or do I get it as a souvenir?"

Lena left the apartment. She walked a few blocks from Ocean Street down to Essex for cigarettes. The cool October wind blew against her, brushing her dress along the inside of her legs. The sensation made her skin tighten up, and for a moment Lena felt that something hard inside her, like the pit of a fruit, might crumble from the pressure.

Lena reached Manoli Meats and Variety where she worked when she was in high school. Now Mr. Manoli was a heavy widower with wide nostrils and tufts of hair that grew out of his ears. He was locking up in his meat-cutting apron when Lena knocked on the glass door. He looked startled and waved her away without realizing who she was but when she knocked again Mr. Manoli recognized her and opened the door a crack.

"You scared me," he said. "I never know who'll come

by after I close. This city keeps getting worse and worse. They rob you during the day now. They throw rocks at your windows."

"I'm sorry, Mr. Manoli." Lena said. "I need cigarettes."

"Come in. Come in." He locked the door behind them. "Catch your breath. What's the matter?"

"I don't know how to tell you this," Lena said. The lights were off at the pastry display counter and the cakes were dim, less sweet-looking than when Lena worked in the store.

"Go ahead, Lena."

"I've got some news for you," she said. Lena's heart slowed and her breath returned to normal. "You're right about the windows. I heard something. Some kids, they were talking about breaking everything, smashing things. I wanted you to know."

This was partly true. She'd heard rumors (but there were always rumors) of a Halloween prank at the beginning of her second-year Spanish class a few weeks ago. Lena softened her voice. "Don't ask me why they'd want to hurt you." The tightness in her skin released, as if she had told Mr. Manoli, of all people, about Eliot and Bert Parks and planting zinnias in Oregon with a woman she didn't even know yet.

Mr. Manoli's forehead turned red and his eyes welled up. Lena sat him down behind the cash register.

"I'll stay with you, right here," Lena said. "I'll keep you company."

After a few more stories, Lena started her business. She came to believe that all sorrows were the same, but she knew the details were different, often complicated, and sometimes she had to go over and over the stories in her mind to make sure she got the information right. Once, a guy who needed to let his wife know about gonorrhea insisted Lena explain that he got the disease from one of those life-size inflatable dolls. He wanted her to say he was drunk and fooling around with the guys, and they were all taking turns banging this plastic sex toy and he had the bad luck to go right after Stan, who left some of his infected semen on the doll. "Anything to keep my wife from her," he told Lena. "She can't know I had real sex."

Lena herself had gone months without real sex until she met Alessandro who was now naked on the bed. Lena studied how his body started out wide at the shoulders, then narrowed near his middle. He had just enough hair, too: a little around the nipples and a neat fan around his crotch.

Sun came through the open window and cast shadows of the grillwork across the floor. It was Friday and Eliot (Ellen, Eleanor, even Elsa, Christ he still didn't know, much like parents don't know the name of the baby until they actually see it) was in the clinic by now. They were shaving him, maybe asking him one last time if this was what he really wanted. Oh, yes, but he did. He'd built his life around this change, bought a house in Kansas with a great big garden. (Maybe, Lena had most recently said, but I can't decide until I see what they've done with you, and I need to meet a few men out there because like it or not I'll have a sex life without you.)

Lena kissed Alessandro on the forehead and he smiled too quickly; he must have been awake, only pretending to sleep. He still had his morning erection. Lean reached to her night stand for hand lotion, squirted some into her palms, and rubbed Alessandro's chest. The lotion turned his body hair light. She worked her hand low and stroked him until he lost his smile to a less deliberate expression of pleasure.

"Shower?" Lena asked, pointing to the bathroom.

"You first," Alessandro said. He put his hands in back of his head and moved his right heel up towards his crotch.

A pigeon was cooing on the ledge outside the open bathroom window (*Columba livia*, page 56). Lena tapped the metal bars to shoo the bird away, but instead it moved closer, as if looking for food. Lena pulled her hand from the window and turned on the shower. Inside, she lathered herself up quickly so her pubic hair was one foamy mass. Lena wondered how good a job they would do on Eliot. She touched herself beneath the foam and felt the complexity of what was there, layer upon layer opening up on itself, like one of those Chinese boxes, one inside the other inside the other; there was a secret somewhere, a secret Eliot and his doctors would never find.

Lena rinsed in cold water. Then, shivering, she stepped onto the glistening white floor tiles where she patted herself softly with the hotel towel. She hung the towel over the window which opened inside like a shutter. It was then that Lena saw the bird had gone, and when she pushed open the bathroom door with her foot, saw that Alessandro had gone, too.

After she dressed, Lena left the hotel and walked to the plaza. More vendors had set up shop where the brother and sister with wooden animals once were. Many sold black pottery and rugs. Others sold cheap plastic toys: whistles, trucks, naked dolls in cellophane bags with flat chests and long eyelashes, Between the legs of these dolls there were no folds to show their sex, just pink plastic, smooth and hard.

"*Cuánto?*" Lena asked. The vendor gave her the price in new pesos, *seis.* Even Mexican money was changing. Now you dropped three zeroes off everything to get the real price.

Lena didn't bargain. She handed the man a bill and a coin that totaled six pesos, about two dollars. She took the doll in the cellophane bag and walked away. Lena looked around for the two children who had sold her the porcupine so she could give the gift to the girl.

It was noon. Clouds had swept in, giving the plaza the look of dusk, or even a solar eclipse. Lena crossed her arms over the plastic doll and held it tight against her chest. She ran to the cathedral behind the vendors where birds now perched above the wooden doors, *Zenaida, Streptopelia* and *Columba,* all the birds she had seen so far in Oaxaca, protecting themselves from the rain. Lena bundled up below them. She heard them all coo in rhythm, like a heart beating. Lena felt a pressure in her head, as if her own heart were beating too hard, and she worked her way into the cold, damp cathedral.

The cathedral was dimly lit by candles that the parishioners bought in exchange for a prayer, a direct line to God. The sign near one section of the candles said the money went to the upkeep of the church. Lena looked around her at the scaffolding for repairs, then back to the candles where a group of girls stood. Their bodies were small, the skin on their faces as tight as their leather sandals. They had the swollen, callused feet of old men.

"Manuela?" Lena asked.

A head turned, but it was a boy's head, Pedro's, who was kneeling in front of the candles. Pedro got up off his knees. He carried a red blanket over his back that he had filled with the wooden toys.

"Hello," Lena said in Spanish. "You sold me a porcupine, remember?"

"Yes."

"This is for your sister." She held out the doll.

Pedro took the gift. He tried to flatten out the doll's long black hair through the plastic.

"Here," Lena said. "Let me fix it." She twisted the doll at the socket around the waist so the legs lined up with the torso. She did the same at the neck, then rubbed a finger over the bag to get some of the wrinkles out. "This is better," she said. She offered Pedro the doll again.

Pedro shook his head.

"What is it?" Lena asked.

"My sister is dead," Pedro said. "You told the truth. We knew that she was sick, but not as sick as your husband. Remember you said my sister looked like he did before he died? You were right. We buried her on the hill near the edge of Oaxaca."

Lena tried to steady her voice before she spoke. "I'm sorry," she said. The rain stopped pounding on the roof and Lena imagined the sky was getting clear again. "Let's go," she said, taking Pedro quickly by the arm.

They walked down the aisle towards the front of the cathedral. Lena tried to keep her mind on life outside, where the vendors were opening up their blankets again and where the birds that had perched above the doors flew away with one magnificent swoosh as Lena and Pedro left the cathedral.

"We'll get something to eat," Lena said.

"I can't eat right now," Pedro said. "I've got these carvings to sell." He broke away from her and headed down the steps of the cathedral towards his usual place in the square.

Lena followed him. "Wait," she said. "I can help you set up. Let me stay with you. Please."

Lena put the plastic doll beside her and held one end of the red blanket to spread it out. Then, one by one, she stood the wood carvings. She stood the turkeys and armadillos, the turtles, the fish and the salamanders. Lena knelt at the edge of the blanket. She stretched her arms around the figures to keep them from blowing over.

"Over there, near you," Pedro said. "I keep all the turtles together, all the fish, too. They face out towards the square." He crawled towards Lena to help her arrange the figures as he wanted them. "There," he said, "and there, and there and—"

*P*edro reached over and grabbed her around the waist. Lena went to hold him, too, but when she tried to move her arms she found that her hands were shaking. She picked up the plastic doll and twisted it, this pink, generic doll that had nothing to do with sex.

Pedro cried out, but the old men in folding chairs had begun to play their music at the end of the square so no one heard him except Lena. She heard nothing but his voice, as if it were in a different pitch from all other sounds, like the call of Mr. Twitchell's rare birds. And this voice, filled not just with Pedro's grief but with Lena's and Eliot's and all the sorrow Lena had delivered these past months, rippled through a placid and distant oasis Lena had guarded inside her. So this is where pain begins, she thought. Here, in another country, until now a place I've never been.

TIPPING COWS

In her later years, after my father died, my mother regained some of her humor and began to play her cholesterol level in the Massachusetts State Lottery. 241, any combination. This was only a faint glimpse of the woman whose bellowing laugh used to set everyone laughing at cookouts and parties. But by the summer of 1973, when I was eleven and the Watergate hearings were on TV every morning, people stopped calling my mother with invitations, even if it meant awkward silences in their small backyards, because to our neighbors any party without my mother was not as much fun. Even then I knew it was my father they weren't inviting, not her, but my mother was the one with the hurt feelings. So she spent that summer watching the Senate hearings. She shook her head and pointed out Sam Ervin to me. "Listen to him," she said. "There is a great man." I suppose I needed a great man in my life to make up for my father, but a senator on TV could never love me. Now all I remember about Sam Ervin is how funny his Southern drawl sounded. My mother was quite taken by him, though, by what she said was his sense of right and wrong, as if he were talking directly to her.

And he was, I guess, because early in August my mother told me it was time that she did what was right and that we were going to finally leave my father and start over again. We drove off one night with a few bags and our pair of diabetic Siamese cats, Mr. and Mrs. Choy, named by my mother. When they had kittens my mother took out an ad to sell them in the *Lynn Item* under the heading MULTIPLE CHOYS. We got phone calls like you wouldn't believe, mostly from people who just wanted to talk to someone who seemed so clever. Now Mr. and Mrs. Choy were blind creatures with glazed-over eyes, creatures that could only eat certain foods at certain times. The night of our escape we pulled into every rest stop on the New York Thruway so my mother could fill their bowls with water and feed them expensive cereal out of her hand.

"You better call your father, Kevin," she said to me at the Syracuse stop. "I'm having second thoughts about this. I left a note that said we got free tickets to the Ice Capades. He expected us back hours ago."

"The Ice Capades? In August? For crissakes." I made sure I dropped the *t* sound in 'Christ' and slurred the two words together.

"He's probably worried sick. Call him collect, OK?"

I had a hard time imagining my father missing anybody. As far as I could tell, he didn't really care for either one of us enough to worry. It was like he was born without a gene that gave you the ability to love.

"We can't call him until we get there," I told my mother.

We were on our way to Canada. We were dodging, just like the boys used to do who refused to fight in Vietnam. I had started to make plans. We would find a place in a small town outside Toronto in time for me to start the sixth grade.

"But we've got your father's car," she said. "How's he going to get to work in the morning?" At that time my father still had his job as an art teacher in the local junior high and was getting his room ready for the fall term.

"Just drive," I said. "Step on it, woman." I took the cellophane wrapper off an expensive cigar I'd stolen at the rest stop. I rolled down the window and blew imaginary smoke into the night air.

"Where did you get that?" my mother said. She looked at me in the rear view mirror. "Who sold a cigar to someone your age?"

"Never mind," I said. I reached down for my Etch-A-Sketch, I shook it clean, then started to turn the drawing knobs.

"I'm warning you," my mother said. "You give me any trouble and we're turning around and heading straight back to Lynn."

"You will like hell," I said. "Get a move on. I'm in charge now."

"You don't talk to me that way," my mother said. She reached in back and swung her right arm in an attempt to hit me across the legs. Our dinky white Nova swerved into the next lane.

"Hey," I said. "You don't have to hit."

"You just behave," my mother said, swinging her arm again. She missed me the second time, but knocked Mrs.

Choy off the blanket. The cat fell on the floor.

"You killed her," I said.

"Pick her up!"

"You iced Mrs. Choy."

My mother slowed into the breakdown lane. I picked up Mrs. Choy. She didn't move.

"Oh, God," my mother said. "Good God. What'll we do?" My mother was crying now.

I put my ear on Mrs. Choy's breast and heard a tiny beat. "Watch this," I said. I pried open the cat's jaw with my index finger and thumb. I cupped her face with my mouth, blew hard, then rubbed little circles around her heart. I bent down and blew again. Mrs. Choy opened her eyes. She shook her head and rolled over. "There you go," I said, slapping my hands together in satisfaction. "Like new."

"That's it," my mother said. "That was a sign. We shouldn't be doing this. I'm turning around. We need to get Mrs. Choy to the vet. She's breathing now, but once we reach Buffalo, anything could happen."

It took me years to forgive my mother for giving up so easily. As we pulled off the Massachusetts Turnpike right before Boston and followed Route 128 to Lynn, I could feel all the strength that had helped me steal cigars and save a dying cat leave me, exit by exit, until we drove up to our front steps. There my father sat, a large, bald and melancholy man, older than my mother by twenty years. His hands were folded on his lap, the thick, soft hands of a painter. He waited for my mother and me to get out of the car and walk up to him before he spoke.

"Where have you been?"

I could tell right away he was in one of his depressions.

The sadness in his voice was so pure that his words rose over me and came back down again, touching my heart as if the sound had originated from some sacred place.

"I'm sorry, Raymond," my mother said. "I'm so sorry. I don't know what came over me." She dropped the Choys and put her arm around my father to help him up. "Tuck in your shirt, Raymond," she whispered. "Zip up your fly. You weren't touching yourself out front here, were you?"

I stayed outside. Mr. and Mrs. Choy walked around the bottom of the steps. The cats bumped up against my legs, then swayed their long black tails to touch what they couldn't see.

"*I* spent most of the summer bringing animals back from the dead," I told the class. It was September, and Miss Natali, a new teacher at our school, wanted us to share our vacations.

"What kind of animals?" Miss Natali asked. She was young and pretty except that none of her teeth were in the right place. She said everything with an eagerness that was supposed to give us confidence.

I took out the cards I had made since the resurrection of Mrs. Choy. I walked up and down the aisles and showed the cards to the class. "You see," I said, "every time I bring an animal back from the dead I draw it on one of these cards." I stopped in front of Miss Natali's desk. "Here we have *before*," I said, holding up a card with a dead pigeon. I flipped the card over. On the other side I had drawn a pigeon flying through the air. "Here we have *after*. I offer these cards as proof."

"These cards aren't *proof*." This was from Kaye, the class brain. "You drew them, Kevin. What do they prove?"

"Now, Kaye," Miss Natali said.

"Kaye, some things you just *know*," I said.

"We should be talking about Nixon and Watergate, not some phony resurrection. Kevin's a fraud." Kaye rolled her eyes.

"Why don't you tell us how you do it, Kevin?" Miss Natali said, her forehead tight with concern.

"Well," I said. "You start out with a dead animal. It has to be recently dead, still warm." I walked around the room collecting my cards. "Take, for example, this raccoon." I showed a card of a raccoon out cold on its side. "All you have to do, if you have the special talent, is open the mouth and blow. Like this." I bent down and pulled Kaye's head back by her long hair. She screamed. Some of the other girls in the class screamed with her, in sympathy, I suppose. Then I put my mouth on hers and blew hard. I stuck my tongue inside. Miss Natali ran to me and pulled me away by the shoulders.

"That's enough," Miss Natali said. She looked around as if waiting for someone to tell her what to do. "We'll have none of that," she went on.

"Give me those cards, Kevin," Miss Natali said. "Now."

My mother and father were called in for a meeting with Miss Natali and the principal. My mother cried. She let out these big heaving sobs that sounded oddly enough like the way she laughed. My father sat with his hands pressed tight against his crotch in such a way that Miss Natali looked down at him a couple of times, then pretended she didn't.

My father was doing even more things like this now. A

few nights before I caught him in just his boxer shorts, spread out across the pool table in the basement. He'd lifted the Choys up there with him. They were walking around him, sniffing and licking the salt off his old skin. My father was touching himself, rubbing his hands over the white hair on his chest and then down between his legs. His eyes were squinted and his brow wrinkled, which made him seem puzzled, like he really wasn't involved in what he was doing. I thought he was squinting because far ahead of him, where I couldn't possibly see, my father knew there was a reason why he was touching parts of himself that shouldn't be touched, not in front of Miss Natali, anyway, or at the dinner table, where he'd taken to gobbling down huge mounds of food in no time, then afterwards he would sit, his head back and his eyes fixed above us, rubbing his fingers under the tablecloth as if doing a secret rosary.

"**M**y mother tries to cheer us up," I told Dr. Sorenson, my psychiatrist. He had blond hair and a Swedish accent. He bobbed his head with his lilting voice. I was in the eighth grade now. I'd gone a long time without touching Kaye, but a few weeks earlier, in the lunch line, I sneaked up behind her, put my orange tray on the floor, and slipped my hand under her arm to feel the newly-formed curve of her breast. This was why I was with Dr. Sorenson.

"And how does your mother cheer you?"

"She collects jokes. She stays up and writes down the best lines in Johnny Carson's monologues, then she tells them to my father and me at breakfast."

"What about your cards?"

"I still have them."

I kept drawing my resurrection cards long after Mrs. Choy died for good. I drew birds, ants, a flounder from Brown's Pond. I found a squirrel splattered on Jenness Street that I couldn't do much for but I drew it anyway, flattened on one side of the card, then, wonder of wonders, three-dimensional and breathing on the other side, an acorn clutched in its paws.

"Do you draw these animals because your father is an artist, Kevin?"

I told Dr. Sorenson that my pictures were nothing like the ones my father did. My father's paintings were still, clear scenes of mountains in Vermont, the state where he was raised by his Aunt Sylvie. I loved the sharp quality to the lines in his work. In his paintings, the colors never ran. Everything was separated from everything else, every part of everything was separate, even the spots on his Vermont cows, like stained glass. I wanted Dr. Sorenson to know this about him.

"The other day I drew a cow on my new set of cards," I told Dr. Sorenson.

"You drew a cow," Dr. Sorenson said.

"That's what I said."

"Kevin," Dr. Sorenson said. "Where did you find a cow to resurrect in Lynn?"

"I didn't say I found it in Lynn," I said. The closest thing to open space we had in Lynn was the Stop & Shop parking lot. "Sometimes I get out of this shithole."

"Where?"

"There are cows in Vermont," I said.

"And you saved them?"

"I did," I said. "Of course."

Nobody ever mentioned that my father had had a nervous breakdown until after he died, and even then I think most of us who knew him had a hard time with that term because it wasn't like he was really breaking down in any major way. What was happening, it seemed to me at least, was that some strange voices nobody else could hear were speaking to him, and in a manner that none of us understood they filled out part of the sad, quiet void my father had with him all his life.

I'm sure there were earlier signs of my father's breakdown. Maybe he overslept too often or kicked the Choys away from his desk with a temper we hadn't seen before. But the first time for certain he went over the top was the night he told me about tipping cows. This was before my mother started to drive to Toronto, or even before the cats went blind.

Late that night my father carried me into the den. We walked past my mother's sewing room where she had a sofa bed. The theme for *The Tonight Show* was playing, and I pictured Johnny Carson sweeping his hand in front of the curtain, ready to step out and tell his jokes.

"We're going cow tipping," my father said. I smelled the beer on his breath.

The TV audience laughed.

"Cow tipping?" I asked.

"Cow tipping," my father repeated. He twisted his callused toes into the thick wall-to-wall carpeting that was the color of cream. "Like me and Aunt Sylvie used to do."

The Choys scratched at my mother's door. My mother clapped for them to get away.

My father said, "We were in Vermont. She'd wake me up in the middle of the night and we'd go out to the field to cow tip. What you do is find some cows that're asleep, then very gently touch them with your fingers like this." My father held up his hands and spread his fingers out wide. "They tip over in their sleep without even knowing it. It's the funniest thing."

"Don't the cows get hurt?" I asked.

"They don't feel a thing. It's the most normal thing in the world." He sat next to me on the sofa. He told me to put up my hands and stretch out my fingers. "Tip me," he said.

"I'm tired, Dad."

"Just once. Aunt Sylvie and I used to do it to each other all the time after we did the cows."

"Dad," I said, wiggling on the sofa.

My father pulled my arms toward him and spread my hands out across his chest. He was wearing a white T-shirt, and I felt his bristly hair. His chest seemed enormous to me that night. He gave me one of his squints like he didn't understand me.

"Push," he said.

When I pushed, my father didn't fall away from me on the couch. Instead, he flopped forward and his head landed on my lap. He slobbered all over my pajamas, rubbing his face right between my legs until I felt a hardness and then a tingling all over me that I thought would make me burst. I put my mind on the cows. They came in different colors, some with beautiful white spots on their backs. Their eyelids were fluttering and their noses were wet. Some cows were bigger than others, but they all fell, no matter what their size. I pictured them gently toppling over. In my mind I stroked their heads and checked their breath to see if they were alive. Often they were bathed in moonlight, and I wondered what they were dreaming.

It wasn't until the spring of my tenth grade year that my father was fired from his teaching job. They said he was acting inappropriately in front of his students, which I eventually learned meant that he touched himself while he talked about the use of pastels in watercolor paintings.

Everyone knew. In the locker room some guys would come up to me on their way to the showers, naked, and reach down to their crotch, or reach over for mine. They left sketches of animals in my books: dead dogs, cats, and pigs, rolled over on their backs, with huge stiff penises in the air, and references to erections, *resurrections.* These boys were clever and had good memories.

Kaye was nicer. She sat with me at lunch a few days after my father was fired, a pile of books between us, and told me that she understood me now and didn't hate me like she used to, even though she still didn't trust me completely.

"You used to have those cards, remember?" Kaye said. "What was all that?"

I forced a laugh and shrugged.

"You don't still have them, do you, Kev? I mean, magic is one thing but you're sixteen years old."

"Of course not," I lied. I really did still have a pile of cards on my bedroom window sill. I'd been taking one off the top and putting it in my bottom drawer every week my father and I went through without cow tipping. I thought that eventually, once all the cards were away from the window and in the drawer, I might be able to believe that we never tipped in the first place.

"But what I don't understand is why," Kaye said. "Why does your father do all those weird things?"

That night, like many nights after my father lost his job, I didn't sleep well. Mr. Choy was still alive but my mother had to feed him with an eyedropper because he couldn't digest solid food. She kept him in a basket right next to her sofa bed in the sewing room. Sometimes my mother would walk around the room at night, Mr. Choy in her arms, tickling between his eyes with her index finger. She sang to Mr. Choy, swaying, her long velour robe sweeping the floor.

I heard Mr. Choy meow inside my mother's sewing room. I hadn't heard him meow for a long time, so I stopped and listened some more, then heard some banging, and my mother's muffled voice asking my father to stop. He'd been going in there more and more since he was fired. My mother had told me we had to support him, that people were out to lay my father off from work because he had so many years tenure and was more expensive than the young teachers coming out of Salem State.

I pushed open the door. My father was spread out over the sofa, his pants around his ankles. I could barely see my mother underneath him, but I heard her crying into his shoulder as he worked her over as fast as he could. He was in such a fever he didn't even hear me in the doorway.

"You fuck," I said. "You don't have to fuck everything in sight, you know."

My mother screamed, but my father just stopped. He rolled off my mother and looked up at me with those squinting eyes of his and this pleading expression on his face. My mother sat up and turned her back on me so I wouldn't see her naked.

"Get out of here," she said. "Get out. Just get out." I stayed where I was. She kept crying for a while and then picked up her bathrobe off the floor to use the ends to wipe her face, Finally, she found it in her to say, "I don't ever want to hear you talk that way." She spoke slowly, the words more an obligation than something she really felt at the time. "Now go." She buried her face in the robe.

"Kev," my father said.

"If you loved us you wouldn't be doing things like this," I said. "Do you even know how to love?"

"I just don't know how to answer something like that." My father dropped his head back and wiped his arm across his eyes. "I'm sorry. I just don't know what to say."

Things did ease up after a while. My father's therapist gave him some drugs that were supposed to calm him down and stop his needing sex all the time. I don't think the doctor gave him nearly enough so my father took to going out at night. The kids at school told me he'd been seen picking up women at strip shows on Route One and the Combat Zone in Boston, and even though I never asked them how they ever found something like that out, I believed them completely, assuming my father wasn't about to change his essential nature after all these years. Besides, I was happy enough that he wasn't touching me or my mother anymore.

My father worked at odd jobs during this time. He made T-shirts and posters he sold to merchants at Salem Willows, and a few days a week he worked on a fishing boat off the Gloucester coast, where he eventually died while I was in my third year at the University of Chicago. I was studying English and trying hard to love a man from Cape Cod who claimed he loved me.

Evan had grown up in England and had an accent that charmed me. He was tall and slender with silky brown hair. It started typically enough: a party, a few drinks, a tense walk to his place. He hugged me before he kissed me; that seemed to clinch things. I felt at home in a way I never felt when I thought about Kaye. Still, it was not easy for me to love a man. The nights of cow-tipping with my father inevitably resurfaced and in the middle of the night I would roll Evan over so he wouldn't touch me while I slept. I had to fight to be who I really was.

It was Boston's coldest December in years when my mother called to say my father had been found in a tiny house that lost its heat during the night. He was in a chair, dead from hypothermia. A man named Jack Simmons, who had hired my father to fish off his boats, discovered him. Jack also owned a small grocery store by the water.

I spoke to my mother on the phone in the hall of my dormitory and was surprised by the sadness in her voice. Over the past years my mother had lost some of her laugh, but she never seemed as unhappy as my father. She'd fixed her life on some safe emotional plane where the highs and lows couldn't touch her. Still, she cried on the phone that day. I hadn't heard her cry since Mr. Choy died.

"We'll have the wake one afternoon and night with the

funeral the next day," she said. "Is that OK with you, Kev?"

"Sure," I said. "Whatever you want."

"Come home."

I drove back from Chicago with Evan. We traveled through the night across Pennsylvania, the sun rising around Scranton where we saw a dead deer on the side of the road. I was tempted to tell Evan about my resurrection cards— it seemed as good an opportunity as any—but as he fiddled with the radio knob trying to find something other than a Christian Fundamentalist broadcast, I decided to allow myself some more time before I let Evan know anything important about me.

"Before we go to my mother's I'd like to stop by Gloucester," I said when we crossed the Massachusetts line around noon. "I want to talk to somebody there, one of the fishermen who might be able to tell me something about how he died."

I pulled off to go north on Route 128 to Gloucester. Jack Simmons' grocery store was red with weather-beaten shingles. Jack was in his sixties, I guessed, and wore a plaid flannel shirt. His skin was tight and dark from the sun and the ocean. He took off his glove and shook my hand when I introduced myself, then he ushered me into his store.

"I can't stay long. I've got somebody in the car," I said.

"I'm sorry about your dad."

"My mother called and told me yesterday. I'm on my way to see her now."

"I wish I'd had a chance to talk to her," Jack said. He poured me some coffee and motioned for me to sit in a high back rocker. A fire was burning in the wood stove. "I might have been able to soften things for her. He had his problems, your dad did, but all in all he was a real quiet guy. Just because I had to let him go doesn't mean I still didn't care about him, you know."

"You fired him?"

Jack was surprised at my question. "You didn't know? I'm sorry. I shouldn't have said anything." Jack lit a cigarette and threw the match into the belly of the stove. "I didn't want to. Really, I didn't. He gave me no choice."

"Then why'd he keep coming back here every weekend?"

"I really don't think I should be telling you any of this," Jack said. "I thought you knew things."

"You found my father," I said. "I need to know." I put the coffee mug on the floor and leaned forward in the rocker.

"OK," Jack said. He sat on the stool beside the cash register and ran his leathery fingers across the counter as he spoke. "I'll tell you as long as you promise you'll never breathe a word of this to your mother. She doesn't need to find out anything she doesn't know already. I'm speaking in confidence, understand?"

"Right."

Jack looked right at me as if he were talking about a business deal. I expected him to tell me my father had been touching himself again in front of people or maybe he stole something or had shown up drunk a few mornings in a row.

"Your father was in love. A local woman a good ten years younger than he was. He met her one of the first weekends he spent here, which is why I ended up letting him go. Love made him unreliable. He wasn't showing up on time. He was missing trips just to be with her. I couldn't have that."

"You're not serious," I said.

"You think I'd just sit here and waste my time making up a story like that?"

"Why should I believe you?"

"Well, you'd better believe me. He had a place rented down by the waterfront. He was with her when he died. His heart just gave out. That woman stayed with him all night. The next day the woman came into my store and told me what'd happened. I went down to the house and found him."

I turned around and looked out the window that was covered with a thick film of salt from the ocean air. It would have been easier for me to hear that my father had been sleeping around with everybody in town and that he was doing it without any discretion at all. That way I wouldn't have had to figure out if he'd always had the potential to love all these years, but that I just couldn't tap it.

"Thanks," I finally said to Jack. "Can I give you anything for your time?"

"Get out of here," Jack said. "I'm not about to take money from you."

I went back to the car and asked Evan if he'd like to go for a walk with me. We made our way down the road to an unbroken view of the ocean, save for the Gloucester Fish Company factory and a spit of land off to the side. Evan slipped his arm into mine.

"The guy in there said my father was in love."

"Your dad was in love, was he? That's good," Evan said. We looked out over the water. Some boats were coming in, boats my father might have been on, his net filled with fish. One of the them tapped into a buoy and stalled there. Jack came out of his grocery, wearing a wool hat with long flaps over his ears and a pair of yellow hip boots. He ran along the dock out into the water and yelled to the men on the boat.

"That happens all the time on the Cape," Evan said. "Even with radar and those buoys and everything. Can you imagine what it was like when they didn't have the equipment we do now? They must have been crashing all over the place."

Jack made sweeping signals with his arms. A rowboat was lowered from another boat. Jack hopped in and headed towards the grounded fishing boat.

"I once heard that when people first landed on places like the Vineyard, they used to throw their livestock overboard to see how deep the water was," Evan said. "They'd heave a horse or a cow right overboard and if it could stand up straight, it was time to anchor. If it tried to swim, then you still had room to travel."

At once I imagined a crowd of settlers struggling to lift a cow over the side of the boat. The cow must have resisted, and more than one passenger would have been kicked hard as the settlers counted *one, two, three* to push the animal in unison. Then the cow would whirl its head around and see the vast ocean for the first time.

"I can't believe they'd go risking their livestock like that," I said. "It doesn't make sense."

"I didn't say I knew for certain," Evan said. He walked away and put his arms along the metal railing of the ocean wall.

I followed him. "I don't know whether or not to tell my mother about my father being in love."

"It's up to you."

"I don't think I will." I said. I didn't think she'd find the same comfort in the story that I was trying to find. In the end, at least, he had shown some tenderness. I had the thinnest of connections to my father's life, but maybe this final act was something I could hold on to, a point where I might for the first time choose to touch him. I held Evan tight against me.

"You might be right," I said. "They could have thrown animals overboard. I'm sorry to be such a skeptic."

Maybe the settlers brought children on the boat who would laugh at the sound of the cow's deep moo. They would run to the edge of the boat just in time to see this cow that was supposed to jump over the moon land in the water instead; then everyone would wait to see if it needed to swim or maybe, this time, they had sailed close enough to the shore to disembark safely, the sacred land firm beneath their feet.

33 1/3

"*I* can squeeze you in after 'Love Child,' Theo, but it's three minutes, tops," Fiona said. Jerry, our producer, was sticking little cue cards in front of her while "You Keep Me Hangin' On" played. It was Supreme Saturday at WHOP, a radio station at the top of an abandoned hotel in downtown Lynn that broadcast throughout Greater Boston. Fiona was nearing the end of her show when she typically played all the biggies like "Where Did Our Love Go" and "Stop in the Name of Love."

"Thanks," I said. "I can take care of this in no time." I looked at Jerry who was now ripping up his cue cards in frustration. He was an old yearbook picture from the fifties brought to life: short hair, black glasses, Oxford shirt with the buttoned collar; a style that might actually look trendy on anyone else these days, a sort of restrained Bohemian aura, *nerd a la mode*.

"Why do we even have a producer?" Jerry asked, throwing the shredded cards in the air. The pieces fell back down on him like the bad stage snow at the Lynn PTA Winter Songfest. "We cannot cancel Sheldon again. He'll be crushed."

Sheldon Jarvis was a retired mailman who had started a petition drive to bring Diana Ross to Lynn. He wanted her to star in a semi-staged *Evita* at City Hall to benefit the local community theater. Jerry had promised him some air time to plead his case but last week Sheldon was bumped so Fiona could interview a man whose niece had seen the Supremes live in concert thirty years ago. There was a call-in segment to the piece, during which the man tended to answer, "Can I get back to you on that? I'll have to ask her at Christmas."

"Don't worry, Jerry," I said. "It won't be more than a minute. Two minutes at the most."

"We just can't send the man home empty handed again. The poor guy's in the bathroom right now combing what little hair he has left before he goes on the air."

I opened the studio door a crack and looked into the waiting room to see how Ian was coping. Ian was the man I thought of as my lover. We'd been sleeping together for a few months, and this was long enough to let my heart begin to shift and settle in with him, like the weakened terrain of an aftershock.

Ian was staring out the window at the afternoon drizzle. The smoke from his cigarette filled up the room, the only place I knew of besides the gay bars where you could still smoke without ventilation.

"You OK?" I asked. I walked up to him and slipped my arms under his from behind. "She's giving me a few minutes. We can go soon. I promise."

I heard Sheldon's nasal voice approach from the hall outside. "But I don't want to give up any of my time," he said as he walked into the waiting room with Jerry. Sheldon was short and heavy-set, and had put on enough cologne in the bathroom to cut through Ian's smoke.

"You'll still get enough time," Jerry said to Sheldon. He patted him on the shoulders to calm him down. "It's just that this is an emergency."

It really was an emergency. I'd come back to WHOP after doing my own show that morning so I could read a description of my Aunt Fran to the listening audience and tell everyone she had just disappeared from her "R.P.M. Day." In my family we celebrated when anyone turned 33 1/3, 45 or 78. It all started with my grandfather, who sold appliances in Wyoma Square well into his eighties. The day my grandmother turned 78, he brought a record player home from the store. The two of them celebrated with their new music and the tradition began. Now Aunt Fran was 78. While my mother pulled out the old gramophone to play an Al Bowlly 78 (this was always part of the celebration, to play the speed that matched your age), Aunt Fran vanished, *poof!*, my mother had said, the same *poof!* she had used years before (I remember this well, the near campiness of it) when she told me the rumor about a woman in Minneapolis who had put her French poodle in the microwave to dry after she washed him and the dog, well, he just *exploded*. "Fifi, *poof!*" she'd said, flapping her hands.

Now Aunt Fran, *poof!*

"I'll call the police. You hurry back to the station and put out an all-points-bulletin," my mother said as soon as I walked into the yard. Ian and I had had a fight on the way to the party so he stayed sulking in the car while I made an appearance. It started that morning when I found my first gray hair, a gray *chest* hair, the first real sign of age. I needed to talk with someone but Ian simply heard me out, yawned, then turned up the radio to listen to Fiona's program. I called him a self-centered bastard who only cared about where his cock went every night, a remark he took personally.

"We'll find Aunt Fran," I said to my mother. "Don't worry."

"But how? I mean, she's too old to be on a milk carton."

My mother clutched my arm. She tended to cling to me more and more in her old age. Sometimes I convinced myself that she had this crazy idea that by touching the life she gave over three decades ago, she might be blessed with a few more years herself. But I knew the real reason she couldn't keep her hands off my body was that she'd fallen madly in love with me when I was thirteen and had never snapped out of it. The night of her retirement party from Sears, her boss brought her up to the microphone to give her a watch. "Dolly, what do you plan to do with the rest of your life?" he asked. My stomach tightened up. In the time it took my mother to spit out the first words, I imagined her smiling wide, an elderly Miss Massachusetts waiting to up-set the blonde from Oklahoma for the crown. *With my husband dead, my son's the only man left in my life. I'd like to touch him as much as possible during my Golden Years. That is, of course, when I'm not making apricot pineapple jam or collecting for the Jimmy Fund.*

Aunt Fran had spent most of her life with Leo, a stingy silent man who worked in the leather factory right over the

Peabody line. My aunt's red hair had faded over the years, despite her monthly dyeing ritual, and was now a pale auburn, as if fifty-five years of married boredom had drained out the color. "Wouldn't you know it?" she said standing over Leo's corpse at the wake. "The first night the two of us are out together in years and he gets the goddamned flowers." A week later—*ah, freedom!*—Aunt Fran started getting out on her own. She wanted to do something passionate and meaningful, she said, so she sat at tables in downtown Boston with people half her age selling T-shirts and bumper stickers for all sorts of causes: U.S. OUT OF NICARAGUA, JESUS ACTED UP, SUBVERT THE DOMINANT PARADIGM. She joined PFLAG, started buying *The Village Voice*, and collected signatures to get prisoners out of jail in Argentina.

"I bet it's one of those urgent action things," I told my mother. "Fran probably had to rush out to do some emergency petitioning or something."

"Please do not treat me like a child. Never forget I am your mother, Teddy," she said, patting me on the butt.

My real name is Theodore. My mother still calls me Teddy, even though I changed it to Theo when I got the job at WHOP so I could name my Saturday morning show "Brio with Theo," three hours of upbeat music, everything from "Carmina Burana" to the Pointer Sisters.

"OK, I'll go to the station," I said. My mother stood on tiptoe and kissed me hard on the lips.

So here I was, watching Jerry hold up ten fingers to Fiona and me to let us know we'd be on the air soon. Fiona took the headphones from around her neck and put them over her ears. Her hair hung long and dark and frizzy. She was wearing an oversize blouse to keep herself cool at the start of her seventh month of pregnancy. Her lover had been sent to jail for something to do with bad auto sales and fraud on the Lynnway.

"Five seconds," Jerry said. He stuck another cue card in front of Fiona that said MARRY ME. Jerry had been in love with Fiona ever since she'd started working at the station, and often put little gifts in front of her mike before she got to work. This morning he'd given her coupons for a dozen roasters at Chicken World right below the station.

"Now," Jerry said, waving his hand.

Fiona introduced me. I explained to the audience that I was missing my aunt, then gave a brief physical description of her. I asked anyone who had information to call the station or the Lynn police. Fiona followed the announcement with "Someday We'll Be Together."

"That should pull on their heartstrings," Fiona said. She leafed through the stack of coupons for the chickens.

"They're easy to serve and fairly nutritious," Jerry said.

Fiona rolled her eyes. "Thanks, Jer," she said, then waved him away. "That guy's been after my ass since I was a fetus." She studied one of the coupons. "*Roast chickens?*" She gave me the same look of horror I remembered when I had come out to her last winter, only at that time she'd softened a bit. "No, actually that's good you're gay," she'd said. "I'm just surprised, that's all. I mean you're so cute, sort of. You'll be hot property, I'm sure. Anyway, I'll remember this moment always. Always, Theo. I'll remember where I was when you told me you were gay."

"Just like people remember when the Kennedys were shot," I'd said. I was born the year after JFK was killed in

Dallas, but I was old enough to remember when Bobby died.

"The Kennedys? I was a child of the Shuttle," Fiona said proudly.

"*Meow*," I said, pulling my hand up like a claw. Fiona knew I was having problems with my age. I hadn't gotten over the anger at having missed my youth because I'd come out so late. I felt as if years ago I'd accidentally thrown away a winning lottery ticket and had to settle for a few cheap victories at a Knights of Columbus bingo later in life.

Dr. Roberta Fleece, my heavy, white-haired therapist who wore wool skirts that seemed to need adjusting whenever I spoke, tried to calm me down by telling me age didn't really matter when it came to sex, nor did looks. "Do you know what the most important sex organ is?" Dr. Fleece asked. I squirmed in my chair. "The *brain*," she said. "Think about *that*." Which I did, for a moment, then, smirking, noted that if that were the case they'd make condoms for your head.

"You're supposed to tell me that thirty-three isn't old, that I haven't missed out on that much in life," I said.

"I never tell you what to think. I help you tell what you think," Dr. Fleece said, slipping her fingers into her waistband.

My sessions weren't making things better. At the bars I'd taken to watching the men who came through the door, one by one. *Older, younger, older, younger*, I whispered, trying to estimate where I stood in the crowd. "Why does young have to be so young?" I asked Ian. "I thought being in your thirties was supposed to be OK, but it's like with everybody dying so early you've got to be in your teens these days to get a head to turn. The median keeps dropping."

At work only Jerry was older than I was, by a year and a half, and Shuttle Child wasn't even alive during Watergate let alone JFK. Right after I told her I was gay, which now seemed decades ago, Fiona jabbed a pencil into her electric sharpener to cover the silence. "And no, Theo, I don't see your coming out as some sort of national disaster, OK?" she finally said, trying to get me to talk again. "Besides, you're not that important, so even if this was something awful, it could never be really bad because it's happening to you. Do you see what I'm saying?"

"I think so," I said.

"Look, I wish I could be more excited," Fiona said. "It's just that, well, I've got problems of my own right now. Look at me, about to have a baby, and my boyfriend's in jail. And I work in *Lynn*, to top it off. In *Lynn*, Theo. An abandoned girl in an abandoned city. I've turned into a fucking metaphor." Fiona sniffed as I handed her some tissues one at a time. "Or am I a simile? I could never get those things straight."

"I don't know," I said. I put down the tissue box and wrapped my long arms around her.

"Anyway, do you have a boyfriend or anything? Is that what you'd call him?"

"His name is Ian," I said.

We'd met through the personal ads in the *Phoenix*. I scribbled the box number from the MEN SEEKING MEN column and left a message. "Supper time sounds great," I said, then left my number. Ian called a week later.

"The ad said *super* times, not *supper* times, bloke."

This guy had a beautiful English accent that made me think he must look like Daniel Day Lewis or possibly Sting.

"Well," I said. "We don't have to have supper, then. Maybe just lunch. Or a snack, maybe? Tea with milk?"

We met the following day at a small health food restaurant on Newbury Street that also sold wind chimes. Ian didn't look at all like Daniel Day Lewis or Sting. He looked more like Anthony Newley, a cross of styles between tweed and grunge. He was about ten years older than I was, and much shorter, and hadn't shaved for a few days, but I still really wanted to see him naked.

"You must be Theo," Ian said. I'd told him I was tall with weight proportionate to my height, a subtle way of letting him know I needed to shed a few pounds. I wore a violet silk shirt that I'd bought at Filene's that morning and black jeans. Ian had said he'd be sitting at a table and that I'd simply know who he was, so he didn't give me a description of himself.

"I told you that you couldn't miss me," Ian said, taking a bite of the scone he'd already started. I called the young waitress to our table and ordered.

"The food here is good for you, *Ian*." I'd read in a *Cosmo* that Fiona left at the station that one way to charm a man was to call him by his first name and look him in the eye as much as possible. "I mean, they don't give you any of that fried greasy stuff that wreaks havoc with your skin, or at least my skin. Yours is just perfect." I gulped, wondering if I'd just said something foolish, then added, "*Ian*."

That very morning, I'd developed a zit right around my left nostril, the kind that only gets bigger by the hour. I dabbed myself with Clearasil at every red light into Boston. After Ian and I made love that afternoon on the shiny wood floor of his South End condo where I could actually see the pimple if the sun was at the right angle, I stroked and kissed him, then tried to fill in the silence.

"Ian," I began. "I want you to know that I'm fairly attractive without acne." Ian rolled over. "Oh shit, Ian, I'm sorry. It's just that, well, this is my first time with a man. Sort of. I mean, there were a few others but I really didn't want it like I do with you. Lately all I do is watch videos, but now I'm bored with them." I wondered how long it took to get bored with sex. For almost a year, since I'd come out, I'd been watching pornos on my VCR, and slowly the thrill had gone to the point where my nightly movie time (11:15, right before Letterman) was part of my going-to-bed routine, like brushing my teeth or my cucumber facial mask. I felt better afterwards, but it took discipline to start every night, and thinking of this that afternoon with Ian, I hoped that real sex didn't end up that way, and that a year later I'd have to find something beyond real sex that was still sex.

I rubbed Ian's shoulder. "Anyway, this was great for me. Really. I hope you enjoyed it, too."

Ian repositioned himself on his back and stared at the ceiling. "I guess you're not without your charm," he said.

"Thank you," I said. When you've gone as many years without a warm body next to you as I have, the praise is never faint enough to damn. But in the weeks that followed I started to understand that Ian would never really love me the way I loved him.

It was like what they say about sleeping with someone, that when you go to bed with somebody you're sleeping with everyone he slept with, and everyone *they've* slept with and on and on. Well, that was me with Ian, in a funny sort of way. Sometimes I felt like I was not just loving Ian, but also all the men I didn't get to love in my teens and twenties, and maybe even all the men *they* didn't get to love. When I found Ian, I was hit with the cumulative emotion of years of lost time.

It all boiled down to this: I wanted all those years back. Every last fucking one of them.

"**I** know Aunt Fran will show up," I said to Ian after I broadcast my announcement. "She's just pulling another stunt." We were taking a walk outside the radio station. A soft drizzle kept us underneath the railroad bridge that led to Boston.

Ian and I stopped in front of Chicken World, which really wasn't much of a world since you could only buy roast chickens inside, nothing else, not even drinks. The windows were covered with a thick film from so much roasting. You could barely see inside the tiny store, and the sign that was supposed to draw people in, GREAT CLUCK FOR YOUR BUCK, was slimy and curled along the sides. I was glad when Ian lit a cigarette because it took away some of the greasy smell that wafted out the door.

"Was that a movie house?" Ian asked, pointing to a boarded-up building on the other side of the bridge.

"For years. Then it became a porn theater for a while, until people got tired of even that. You know your city's dead when it loses interest in smut. I mean, smut is the last to go."

When I was in high school, I sneaked into that theater to watch the naked men in the movies. Gay porn was impossible to find in Lynn, so to fill the gap I used to hit the Capitol or cut and paste the men in the straight hard-core sex magazines to make my own couples, leaving the women in shreds on the floor, breasts and mouths and legs scattered about my room: my Picasso years. And all the while I'd bring home girls for supper and kiss them horribly, second- and third- and fourth-rate kisses, never the real thing. Sixteen years of low-fat ice cream and trying baseball games.

Ian moved away from Chicken World and was now leaning against a pillar that supported the bridge. A train went by and I had to wait before I spoke so I wouldn't have to shout.

"I can't believe mine is next," I said.

"What are you talking about?"

"My R.P.M. Day. 33 1/3. I have mine in a few months," I said. "All my life I've seen people in my family have their R.P.M.'s. They always seemed so old to me. Now it's my turn, Ian." I reached into Ian's shirt pocket and pulled out the pack of cigarettes. "Light me," I said when I'd stuck one in my mouth. Ian leaned towards me, ready to light me with his own cigarette. At the last minute I threw my cigarette away, took Ian's out of his mouth, and kissed him hard.

"What are you doing?" he asked, trying to squirm out of the kiss.

"What does it look like I'm doing? I'm kissing you in public. My first time ever." I pulled him towards me again. This time he didn't resist, but he didn't help much, either.

"That felt good," I said.

"Jesus," Ian said. "Someone could see us. I don't think people in this city would be too accepting of a couple of faggots making out on their streets." He lit another cigarette.

"It still felt good," I said. But it was the type of good I often experienced when I did something gay for the first time, like dance with a man or buy a present for Ian or go into Glad Day, the gay bookstore in Boston. Just as I was feeling dizzy with freedom, the pain and rage of lost time would surface and start to pull me back down again. I wondered how many years it took to completely air out the closet I had lived in most of my life, even if its doors were now burst wide open, *off its hinges*, I'd told Dr. Fleece. *I won't be happy until these closet doors are blown off their fucking hinges.* She snapped at her waistband when she heard me say *fucking*, as if the sound might erase the word from the air.

"Look, Theo," Ian said. "We have to talk."

"OK," I said. "I'll shut up about feeling old. I promise."

"I think we should re-evaluate our relationship. Breaking up isn't such a bad idea for you, you know. This is only your first real love affair." Ian put his hand on my shoulder to comfort me. His touch was already cold, not even that of an ex-lover let alone a lover, but more a scout master, making the little Webelo feel better that his car had come in last in the soap box derby.

I pulled away from Ian and started back toward Chicken World. I watched the rain come down harder. Most rain, like in the country or even Peabody a few miles away, seemed clean and brought out the freshness in the world, if not now, at least later, after the storm. In Lynn, rain was just one more thing to hide from.

Ian threw his cigarette in a puddle and followed me. "It's just getting too much for me," he said. "Maybe we can see each other in a few weeks if I miss you. You never know. Stranger things have happened." Ian's cocky grin allowed him to say terrible things and pass them off as jokes.

"Hey, you guys!" Fiona was walking towards us under the bridge. She took Jerry's light blue windbreaker off her head that had been protecting her from the rain. "They found your aunt. Your mother called right after my show ended. They found her at McDonald's on the Lynnway."

"Want me to go with you?" Ian asked.

"Whatever," I said. I tried to imagine what it might be like to say yes or no right now and really mean it, committing myself to something more than *whatever*, to just getting by.

"Let's go, boys," Fiona said. "I'll tell you about it in the car."

She was sitting on top of the Golden Arches.

"Well, not on top, actually," Fiona said as we rode down the Lynnway in my beaten blue Mazda. Ian had decided to come with us and was sitting in the back. "She's between the arches," Fiona went on. She twisted her rearview mirror towards her so she could touch up her lips. "Right near where they post the number of hamburgers served, which is still pretty high up. Your mother's afraid she might jump."

They had been changing the number that morning and it had started to rain, so the men—there were two of them, one to attach the new numbers, another to hold up the ladder—left their job with the ladder in place. Apparently Aunt Fran saw the men leave as she was riding by in a cab. She stopped the cab, got out and climbed up.

A crowd had gathered by the time we arrived, about twenty or so people in a clump against the side of the building to keep out of the rain, all staring up at Aunt Fran. The blue bubble on top of the cruiser flashed against their faces.

My mother ran over to me. "Oh, Teddy," she said. "Help, honey. You've got to help her get out of this mess. Every time she sees somebody heading for the ladder she threatens to kick it so we can't reach her."

"Will you look at her?" Fiona said as she pointed up. Aunt Fran was sitting with her legs dangling over the sign, like a young girl on a swing. Fiona had put Jerry's windbreaker over her head again to keep from getting wet. My mother inched towards her to share the jacket. "Please join me," Fiona said.

"Thanks," my mother said, smiling. "You must be Fiona. I'm Dolly. I listen to you on the radio all the time. Teddy's told me all about you. He's my son, you know."

"Excuse me, girls," I said. "But we have an elderly relative who's about to fail her audition for Ringling Brothers if we don't do something soon."

"OK, OK. Teddy, you try climbing up and talking some sense into her," my mother said. She turned back to Fiona. "Well, I just want to tell you I think it's terrible what's happened to you, Dear, with child and all. You'd think your boyfriend could have waited a few years before he decided to get himself sent up the river. Now, if you could pry my Teddy away from that snotty piece of English royalty—*that* would be a match. Don't give up on my son, sweetheart."

"Aunt Fran?" I said. "Do you think you might let me come up and have a chat with you?"

A cop came up next to me and stood. "Don't scare her, whatever you do, Teddy."

"Theo. My name's Theo."

"Well, buddy, that's not what your mother said," the cop shot back.

"Come up if you have to," Aunt Fran said. "But just you, nobody else. Right?"

"Go ahead," the cop said. "Take it nice and slow."

I climbed slowly up the ladder. The rungs were wet from the rain and I slipped a little halfway up.

"Teddy!" my mother screamed from below.

"He says his name is Theo," the cop said.

"Don't you tell me my son's name. Teddy, are you OK?"

"I'm fine, Ma." I continued up the ladder until I reached Aunt Fran. I found some space and nestled next to her on the Golden Arches. "So," I said. "What's this all about?"

"I'm wet," Aunt Fran said. "I'm going to die of pneumonia."

"What are you doing up here?"

"Do you have anything dry? I need to wipe my glasses."

I handed her my handkerchief. "Well?"

"Bunch of constipated old hags," Aunt Fran said.

"What are you talking about?"

"At my R.P.M. party. I just couldn't take it anymore. I had to get out of there, so I sneaked through the house and called a cab and met it down by the Store 24. I was going nuts. Everybody was talking about how sad it was that your Uncle Leo wasn't around for my big day and I'm thinking what the hell are you talking about? Being married to that guy was the worst fifty-five years of my life." Aunt Fran finished drying her glasses and put them back on. "Where's Ian?"

"We had a fight. That's why I was late for your party. I think we're through," I said. It wasn't so hard to say sitting high above everybody in the rain. I suspected it would be much harder to repeat once I was back to earth.

"Did he leave you?"

"Not really. He came with me to see you today."

"Well, if I were you I'd just love the hell out of him until he goes," Aunt Fran said. "Don't give up for a minute."

"I don't know," I said, shrugging. I dropped my head a little and crossed my ankles.

"Look, he came here with you, didn't he?" Aunt Fran asked. She touched my cheek and smiled. "Why don't you call down to him and ask him why he came with you? Give him a chance to say something really romantic out here with all these people."

"Oh, I couldn't do—"

"Go ahead."

"Ian?" I called. He was standing by the glass door to restaurant. "Ian, why'd you come here with me today?"

"Because I was hungry," Ian said.

"See?" I said to Aunt Fran. "It's hopeless."

"Give him time," Aunt Fran said. She let out a deep breath and at once seemed older to me, like all the tension that was holding her body up had leaked out of her, a puncture in an inflatable doll. Her shoulders sagged and her voice became quiet. "You know, I'm beginning to think I'd have been better off spending my life with a good woman."

"That's a nice thing to say," I said. "You've always been so sweet, even when nobody else wanted to come near me."

"You think I'm kidding?" Aunt Fran said. "I'm not being sweet, Theo."

"Then what are you telling me?" I asked. I swung my leg up from the side and tucked my knee up near my chin.

"What do you think?"

"Wow," I said. "That's really great."

"Great?" Aunt Fran said. "I guess so. But I'm 78 years old. Why the hell do you think I asked the cabbie to pull over when I saw this spot?"

"You mean you were really going to jump?"

"Oh, I don't think I was ready to go that far," Aunt Fran said. "It was like something Act-Up would do, I guess. Those guys'll do anything to get attention, let people know they're still here. I suppose I was doing the same thing, just working out my frustrations."

I went to reach for Aunt Fran, but stopped when I heard Fiona call from below. "Hey, you guys, please let me up there. Look who's coming and I don't want to deal with him anymore today. I had to sneak out of the station to even come here."

Jerry had already gotten out of the car and was heading towards Fiona. "You've got to get inside, Fiona," he was yelling. "You're going to get sick and harm your baby."

Fiona held tight as she climbed. I turned myself around and locked my legs around it to keep it steady. I grabbed Fiona's hand when she reached the top.

"That's it. No more," Aunt Fran said. "Here we go!" She pushed the ladder away so it fell to the ground. The crowd screamed when the top of the ladder crashed against the pavement. Aunt Fran gave a little laugh. "Don't you love it? I'm starting to feel better already."

"Thank you, you guys," Fiona said. She wriggled herself between Aunt Fran and me. "It's just that he's been sticking to me like Elmer's glue all day. I can't take it anymore." Fiona looked out over the miles of used car lots, fast food restaurants, the abandoned drive-in, the swamp land. "I've never seen the Lynnway like this," she said. "Nice view."

"Fiona!" Jerry yelled. He stood directly under us now and was looking up with his arms outstretched. "Come down, Fiona, and marry me!"

"Christ," Fiona said. "Will you just hold your fucking pants, Elmer?"

"Elmer?" Jerry said.

"Glue or Fudd. Take your pick." Fiona dropped her head on my shoulder. "Hey, where's Ian?"

"Eating," I said. "He came with us to eat."

"That bad, huh?" Fiona said. "I thought I picked up some tension in the car."

"Well, I told Teddy he shouldn't give up," Aunt Fran said. "You never know. The boy could come around."

"Don't worry, Theo," Fiona said. "You're not that old. You'll find somebody else if Ian leaves. I should be so lucky. You know, I probably will end up marrying Jerry. I just want to make sure I don't have a future first." Fiona rested her hands on her stomach. "Besides, I'll always have Rita."

"Rita?" I asked.

"Oh, yeah. It's a girl. Didn't I tell you?"

"Congratulations," Aunt Fran said. "That's beautiful."

"Hey, she's moving around," Fiona said. "Feel, Theo." She took my hands and placed them on her belly.

"Teddy!" my mother called. "You play your cards right and that child could be yours, you know. Listen to me, OK?"

"Theo!" Jerry yelled. "Don't you dare press too hard! If I play my cards right that child could be *mine!*"

"You feel, too, Aunt Fran," Fiona said.

"That's wonderful," I said. "I'm really happy for you."

"It's sort of cool, isn't it?" Fiona said. "Drop your head down, Theo. Sometimes you can actually hear her, too."

Slowly, I lowered my head so my ear rested gently on Fiona. I put a finger in my free ear to block out the mumbling of the crowd and the sound of the rain. I peeked up at Aunt Fran, who blew me a kiss. Maybe she'd find somebody for herself, even at the age of 78. Who knew? And maybe Ian wouldn't leave me or even if he did, I might meet somebody, too. Me, the man who was not without his charm.

I listened to the baby move inside Fiona. "Wow," I whispered. Then, I swear, I heard Rita's heartbeat, the soft and distant thump of life.

MARIPOSA

"I don't want to be Jolene or Jocelyn or even Josephine," Joey said to his uncle. "I want to be Flo."

"Flo?" Vincent said. His arms were tired. He dropped Joey's heavy canvas bag on the floor, then pushed it with his foot across the threshold of the guest room.

"I'm looking for a whole new image," Joey said. "Right down to my toes." He flipped off his *espadrilles* to reveal red-painted nails. He was wearing earrings, tight jeans without a fly, and a long chiffon scarf wrapped several times around his neck.

"This will be your room," Vincent said. "Towels are in the bottom drawers and if you need a blanket it's under the bed. There's a little TV in the closet, if you want to watch *Oprah*."

"Actually, I'd like to *be* Oprah," Joey said.

Joey spoke more deliberately than Vincent remembered. He seemed to move more intentionally, too, like the way he slowly put his finger to his lips as he surveyed the room. He reminded Vincent of one of the happy home buyers his mother used to watch Sunday mornings on *Builder's Showcase*.

Vincent watched Joey unzip the canvas bag. A few years ago, Joey would have packed sweat socks and a jock strap. Today he took out skirts and nylons. He lined everything up neatly along the end of the bed.

"Thank you for letting me stay here," Joey said. "It sure beats staying in Maine with Mom. She's still pretty freaked out about all this."

"The other day she told me the whole situation reminded her of how she lost your father," Vincent said.

"How's that?"

"She said the two of you both left her for another woman."

Vincent didn't tell Joey that as Louise said this, she was crying.

*L*ouise phoned her brother that afternoon to see if Joey had arrived safely. Vincent was stretched out on his bed, staring at the dust that had accumulated on the blades of the ceiling fan. He was imagining the check list of things he needed to do today: write a check list, do laundry (whites), organize his top desk drawer, rearrange his classical music collection by era rather than by composer.

"I can't thank you enough for taking Joey in," Louise said. "You're a real saint."

"That's not true," Vincent said. "I sometimes forget to recycle, for one thing."

"Maybe this'll be good for you, too," Louise said. "The two of you can keep each other company."

Joey's therapist had told Louise that he needed some time wearing women's clothes, as a warm-up, to see if he wanted to make the change for good. You don't do things like that in Maine, Louise had said. People even stared at her when she wore a dress.

"So how does Joey look to you?" Louise asked. "Did he have anything to eat on the bus? I think he's lost weight. I worry about those hormones he takes."

"Joey looks like Joey, I guess," Vincent said. "Only less so."

"Please don't tell him I called already," Louise said. "I don't want him to think I'm checking up on him."

"OK," Vincent said. "We'll talk soon."

"I love you for this," Louise said.

Vincent hung up and saw Joey standing in the bathroom doorway wearing a pink satin robe. The skin below his neck was smooth now that all his chest hair was gone. Vincent thought that if he touched the robe and Joey's body, the textures might feel nearly the same. Joey slid his robe off, then sat at the edge of the tub, running his hands over his thighs. When he crossed his legs, it looked like all Joey had below was a triangle of dark hair.

Joey went to bed early that night, so Vincent made himself his usual cup of hazelnut coffee. Months ago, he'd come up with the idea of marking two levels of the inside of the cup in permanent, non-toxic paint: one line for coffee level, one for 1% milk. No more guesswork.

Now Vincent sat at his desk. He'd become a translator because he was attracted to the idea of one word meaning another, as if exchanging currency. If there was poetry in the world, it was a poetry of metaphors, where something *equaled* something else; nothing was ever merely like another thing. He liked wearing his T-shirt that said SILENCE = DEATH not so much for its politics, but because the clarity of the message comforted him.

Vincent studied the passage before him from *Butterflies: A Beginner's Guide* that he was translating into Spanish for the Audubon Society:

> No animal sees a greater transformation into adulthood than the butterfly. The metamorphosis from caterpillar (or larva) into the mature *Lepidoptera* is nothing short of extraordinary. Larva can resemble everything from bird droppings to snakes but, remarkably, has no similarity to the winged insect it will become.

Vincent typed the paragraph into his computer. He studied the Spanish word for "butterfly"—"*mariposa*"—then said it aloud, letting the penultimate syllable roll slowly off his lips. Vincent loved translating. Still, he worried at times. He knew memory slipped with age, and even he, only in his mid-forties, had started to forget a word now and then. It was only a matter of time before he'd be using his *Gran Larousse Dictionary* at every turn.

Vincent flipped on the Internet and found one of the

chat rooms for gay men, but there wasn't much action: an older man named Cal was telling a teenaged boy from Jamaica Plain what it was like to see some of the musical stars of the fifties and sixties, like Zero Mostel in the original *Forum*. Vincent didn't want to interrupt, and couldn't find any other men on line. Things didn't heat up on Saturdays until after one or so when all those men who came home alone needed someone to talk to.

Vincent changed into his new khakis and left Joey a note: "In case you should get up and wonder where I am, I've gone two-stepping at Arlington Street Church. Uncle V."

Vincent had come out when he was forty. For a while, he'd go to the bars and stand on the sidewalk, not daring to enter. What was he expected to say to the men inside? He started picking up *Bay Windows*, and read that Arlington Street offered a smoke-free, alcohol-free, safe space. It sounded easier, and after three Saturdays of wandering around outside the church, he finally followed a small group of men through the door.

Tonight Vincent paid his five dollars to Walt, an older, hunchbacked man who never danced but just sat back and smiled while the boys did the El Paso, the San Antonio Waltz, or the Oilcan Slide. Vincent leaned against the wall and listened to the Mary Chapin Carpenter song the DJ had just put on. The men wore cowboy hats and buffed leather boots and seemed to glide across the floor, as if on ice. Whenever Vincent danced, he couldn't glide: He felt barefoot at the beach with scorching sand. Where was his style? He'd begun to think that he wasn't really gay after all. Maybe he was just "ga-," or, worse still, just a "g-"

"Care to dance?"

It was Mr. Chicago, the fifty-something bald taxidermist who came to the dances in the same brown sports coat, a white shirt, and a UNICEF tie with smiling children's faces. He'd told Vincent his first name when they'd met months ago, but all Vincent remembered from the conversation was that the man was originally from Chicago. Mr. Chicago often came at 7:00 to set up, danced every single song, then helped put the folding chairs away at the end of the night.

"I'll lead," Vincent said.

"I saw you standing there all by yourself," Mr. Chicago said. "You should be more outgoing. You have things to offer."

Vincent tried to find the small of Mr. Chicago's back to help direct him to the music. He remembered to whisper the beat into his ear so that he could follow. *Quick, quick, slow, slow. Quick, quick, slow, slow.*

As he spun Mr. Chicago, Vincent wondered how his life turned out this way. Wasn't he supposed to build an entire future around his one big declaration of coming out? In middle age, he felt he was given a credit card without a spending limit, but the only stores he could shop in had just had major liquidation sales. He had to choose from what was left over: the ceramic lawn squirrel with the chipped ear or the golf-green pants the size of a pup tent.

"Thank you," Mr. Chicago said when they finished. He wiped the sweat of his brow with his handkerchief.

"Thank you," Vincent said.

"How can you be sure about this?" Vincent asked Joey after he'd returned the following Saturday night, his first out on the town since coming to Boston.

Joey sat on Vincent's sofa massaging his feet. He wore a tight, short skirt, heels, and a transparent blouse that revealed a white lace bra.

"I just know," Joey said. He ran his ankle bracelet through his fingers. "Right now in my life it's just about the only thing I really do know."

"You've never not known?" Vincent asked.

"I guess I can remember the earliest time I felt this way, but I also know there were times before that. I've just forgotten them, that's all. I don't think you can remember exactly when you knew you were attracted to men, can you?"

"I guess you're right," Vincent said. "Are you attracted to men?"

"Very much," Joey said. "I just don't want to be one anymore. And technically, I'm a male right now. But emotionally I've always been a woman. A real woman. I'll be a total woman after my gender reassignment."

Vincent thought about the word *reassignment*. It sounded so simple, really, as if Joey merely had to make up his math homework.

"I'm sorry if I ask too many questions," Vincent said. "I feel like I've lived on another planet for years and have been plopped down in a new world where all the rules I've spent a lifetime learning have changed."

"It's OK," Joey said. "I want you to understand me."

"If you want to know the truth, I find it sort of exciting, the way you're changing your life. I envy you."

Vincent saw the lamp shine right through Joey's blouse. His bra was perfectly shaped and gleamed in the light. Vincent closed his eyes for a moment so as not to stare, then forced himself to look at Joey's face again. His lips were soft

red, his skin slightly blushed. His long, dark lashes drew
Vincent to his blue eyes. Vincent couldn't imagine Joey looking any other way right then.

"You're very beautiful," Vincent said.

"How's Joey?" Louise asked Vincent on the phone on a
sweltering afternoon the following week.

"You mean Flo?" Vincent said. "I try to think of him as
she now."

"I'm not quite ready to have a daughter yet, even theo-
retically. Humor me for a few minutes and talk about my
son, will you?"

"OK," Vincent said. "Joey."

"Thanks," Louise said. Her voice softened. "I don't mean
to snap. You've been wonderful. It's just that I talked to him
the other day and couldn't get a thing out of him."

"He's young. He's not supposed to communicate to his
mother."

"I guess." Louise sighed. "How is he, Vincent? I want
the truth."

"He looks OK. He bought some more clothes yesterday. Filene's Basement was having a sale."

"God, do you think he tried the clothes on right there?
In the women's dressing room? With all those people
around?"

"I don't know. I'm not sure anyone would have noticed. When he's dressed like a woman, he looks like a
woman."

Louise began to cry. "Christ, this is so hard. I want to
be a good mother. Really, I do. Tell me something good,

Vincent. I need to hear that something's going right for him down there."

"Don't worry," Vincent said. "He knows people now." Joey had made friends in Boston who visited once: Stella, Lauren, Cynthia, Nell.

"Really? I'm glad to know he's not all alone. What are they like?"

Vincent had only said hello to them as they were going into Joey's room. They'd spent an hour or so in there with music playing. Vincent pictured them smoking dope with the window cracked open or helping each other get ready for their big night out.

"They seem nice. They all laugh a lot," Vincent said.

"I'm glad somebody's laughing," Louise said. "How does he look, Vincent?"

Vincent thought about Joey's breasts and how he'd gotten giddy with excitement yesterday when he had to buy a bra that was just a little bigger than his first. The hormones were slowly working. When was the last time Vincent was giddy about anything?

"He's filling out," Vincent said. He put his hand on his own bare chest. His muscles were not as solid as they were in his twenties, but were still strong enough to protect his heart.

"**M**aybe we could exchange numbers," Mr. Chicago said as the last song wound down. He and Vincent were leaning against the wall beside the pass-through in the church basement where popcorn and Arizona Iced Tea were sold.

"Oh, that's all right," Vincent said.

"No, really, Vincent," Mr. Chicago said. "You've got to get more confidence in yourself. I think I could help you. I'm used to working with people."

"But you're an taxidermist."

"So."

"I'm really very busy these days," Vincent said, heading towards the door. "But thank you."

"Live around here?"

"It's quite a walk."

"I'll walk with you," Mr. Chicago said. When he smiled, only his top lip moved, displaying only his top row of teeth.

Vincent tried to hustle ahead, but Mr. Chicago tagged along.

"How long have you been dancing?" Mr. Chicago asked.

Vincent tried not answering but then felt uncomfortable with the silence. "A couple of years."

"Really?" Mr. Chicago said. "I'm a three-year veteran. I don't think I even noticed you until a few months ago."

"That's only because I've never really been a regular," Vincent said.

They walked for a while until Vincent stopped at the Starbucks at the end of Charles Street.

"This is where I leave you," Vincent said.

"Don't I even get a kiss or anything?"

Vincent offered his hand, then headed towards Beacon Hill, almost running.

"See you next week," Mr. Chicago yelled.

When Vincent got home, he went to his desk and flipped on the computer. He opened the book on butterflies:

The third stage in the development of the butterfly is the chrysalis,
which is enclosed in a silk case or co-
coon. Several adult features such as
eyes and antennae are recognizable if
the chrysalis is carefully studied. For
many years, scientists thought the case
served to shape the butterfly, but we
now know the change in form starts
from within.

What if I never change? Vincent thought. What if ten
years from now I'm still the sort of man Mr. Chicago follows
home at night? Vincent didn't want to believe that who he
was now was all that he'd ever be.

"**I** need your help," Vincent told Flo a few nights later.
It was the Fourth of July, Flo's nineteenth birthday. Vincent
had invited her to dinner and a movie, or dinner and a show, or
just dinner—whatever Flo wanted, Vincent said. She'd decided
on dinner, then the two of them would meet Flo's friends down
by the harbor for the fireworks display.

"What can I do for you?" Flo asked. She was finishing
her mascara in front of her make-up mirror.

"I want to try it," Vincent said. "I want to be somebody
else, or at least more like somebody else, just for the evening,
but I can't do it alone."

"This isn't play acting, you know," Flo said.

"Please," Vincent said. "I'm tired of who I am. Maybe if
I can pull something like this off, I can pull off other things,

too. I could change my life." For a moment Vincent pictured what this new life might hold for him: Saturday nights at Chaps or Luxor, maybe a first novel, lovers. "Tonight will be like one of those bungie jumps. Once I take this leap, I'll be daring enough to try anything."

Flo smiled and rolled her eyes. At that moment Vincent thought she was behaving like a typical teenaged girl. She got up from the chair and motioned for Vincent to sit down. "Take off your shirt."

Flo sat beside Vincent and applied some light base. She worked quietly and slowly, looking down at the colors of her Pupa Kit, then up again at Vincent's face, as if painting on a canvas. Vincent closed his eyes while Flo used her thumb to gently blend the colors on his skin.

"There," Flo finally said, adjusting the blonde wig on Vincent's head.

Vincent looked in the mirror. He had to look harder now for the slight groove in his cheek from teenaged acne, the soft lines of age that fanned out from the corners of his eyes, the flaking that sometimes made his lips sore.

"Almost new," Vincent said.

Flo put two skirts with elastic waist bands and some matching blouses on the bed. Vincent picked blue. He thought it would look nice with his blonde hair.

"What about my breasts?" Vincent asked.

"We'll try this for now," Flo said. She took out some nylons from her top drawer and rolled them in two little balls. She handed Vincent a bra. "I've grown out of this."

Vincent dressed with Flo's help. He was surprised at how light everything felt. The silkiness of the panties felt cool against his skin, and the blouse was looser than any shirt he'd ever worn.

"Time to go," Flo said.

At first Vincent walked hesitantly in Flo's slightly too big heels. He felt as though he were in someone else's apartment he'd never visited before. He touched a doorknob differently. He saw the way the sun had faded his books as if for the first time. He was more aware of his posture; he pulled in his belly and stroked it to feel how flat it was, then moved his hand slowly up to his nylon breasts. He tried gently swinging his hips as walked out the door.

"**W**hen he danced with me, I could smell the formaldehyde on his fingers," Vincent said in the restaurant.

"So are you going to go out with him?" Flo twirled her fork in the spaghetti. "He sounded harmless on the phone."

Flo had answered when Mr. Chicago called Sunday afternoon. He invited Vincent to go two-stepping at the Ramrod sometime. Vincent said he would get back to him.

"Too much of my life is already harmless," Vincent said.

Vincent tilted his head so he could see his reflection in the large mirror with the gilded frame opposite him. His wig was still on straight and his pearls hung evenly across his chest. He wasn't very attractive as a woman. He was almost attractive, but not quite, just like most people. A slightly different nose, smaller ears, lower cheekbones—little changes here and there made the difference between average-looking and beautiful.

Vincent put down his glass of red wine. "Do you think I've disappeared, Flo?"

"What do you mean?"

"For me Joey's gone. I hardly think of him anymore. I've tried, the last few days. I got some of your baby pictures just to see what you used to look like. You're standing by a pool stark naked, a tiny sprout of a penis sticking out between your legs. But it's not the same person, is it?"

"It's the same person," Flo said. "Just different packaging."

"I guess," Vincent said. "But what about me? Do you think of me as your Uncle Vincent in women's clothes? Or does the new packaging fit me so well that you don't see your uncle anymore?"

"I just think of you as fabulous," Flo said with a wink.

"Ha-ha," Vincent said. "I don't believe you."

After Vincent paid the bill, they went to the subway stop and boarded a train. An elderly woman in a turquoise shift stared at him. Did he really look that odd? She should have been staring at other people, like the short man at the end of the car who handed out The Lord's Prayer on light blue cards, then swept through again demanding a dollar or the card back, using his hands as a deaf person would. Like the heavy woman who sat with a bucket tipped upside down between her legs, which she banged in short, dramatic spurts, then looked up to the florescent lights, as if expecting rain. Like Flo, who stood next to Vincent but who didn't seem to be a focus of attention, because, after all, Flo was being Flo, not somebody else.

The woman crossed her ankles, her eyes still on Vincent. She knows what she sees really isn't me, Vincent thought. He was glad when the doors of the train opened. The woman was making him feel like a failure. Shouldn't a great translator makes the words seem his own?

Outside, Vincent was surprised there wasn't a crowd. A few people hung around the entrance, but the thousands of spectators the TV news had predicted had moved closer to the ocean, away from the subway stop.

"Look!" Flo yelled to Vincent.

Vincent saw a rocket rise from the harbor, then burst open into a million gold lights.

"Hi, Flo!" Vincent recognized one of the women who had visited Flo at the apartment. "Happy birthday! We've been waiting for you."

Behind her were six or seven other women. Flo hugged her friends, kissing them on the lips as if she hadn't seem them in years.

One of the women introduced herself to Vincent as Sophie, then kissed Vincent quickly on the lips, too.

"Oh, I almost forgot," Flo said to Sophie. "I'd like to introduce you to—"

"Flo stopped mid-sentence and raised her eyebrows, waiting for a cue from Vincent.

"Mariposa," Vincent said.

"How exotic," Flo said. "The Lovely Miss Mariposa."

Vincent looked up where it was dark and calm, all anticipation. He wondered about the colors, the size, the design of the next flare. There was so much he didn't know. He didn't know the names of all these friends of Flo's, or how many of them had already been reassigned, or if among them there might have been someone who was born female. And Vincent didn't know if Flo would stay Flo forever or return to Joey one day, or if, after tonight, he'd say good-bye to The Lovely Miss Mariposa, whoever she was.

A rocket went up with its loud, hollow sucking sound.

"I hope it's the kind that rains down in little spirals," Flo said.

"The ones that look like twirling sperm," Vincent said.

Flo laughed. "You go, girl!"

What would burst above them? Vincent wondered. He smiled at Flo as the cool breeze from the water brushed the dress against his legs.

THE NEAR OCCASION

I'm standing in the water with my lover, Jared, my sports coat over my shoulder and my trousers rolled up to my knees, waiting to dump my mother's ashes into the Nahant Coast. The sun beats so hard it heats the urn and burns my fingers. It's time. I tip the urn upside down and watch a few ashes drop out. My mother was a small woman, but wasn't she bigger than this? I bang the urn hard with the side of my hand. The rest of my mother falls out just in time for a wave to wash her all over me.

"Shit," I say. Only Jared can hear me out here. About fifteen neighbors, cousins, aunts and uncles stand on the beach with Toby, our four-year-old Peruvian son. The retired policemen are there, too, the City of Lynn's former finest and my mother's admirers. The old police caps they've dug out of their closets look funny with the Hawaiian shirts and bright shorts they wear.

"Let me help you, Andrew," Jared says. With his handkerchief, he wipes some of the ashes off the front of my shirt.

"Screw this," I say. I hand Jared my coat and the empty urn. I plunge into the water, then resurface, shaking my hair dry. I open my arms wide so Jared can get a good look at my shirt. "Well?"

"She's gone," Jared says. "Not a trace of her."

When we return to the beach, Aunt Ella, my mother's sister, is holding Toby. My aunt's tiny build somehow makes her all the more powerful, as if she's spent her entire life cultivating inner strength to compensate for her lack of physical stature. She hands me Toby, who holds the visor of his Red Sox cap between his teeth. His skin is moist and shiny from the sun block I rubbed on him this morning.

"I really think your father should have come," Aunt Ella whispers to me. "It's the least he could have done."

"I haven't talked to him in years," I lie. "There's no way he would know."

"I'm so sorry, but it really is a blessing," one of the policemen interrupts, patting me on the shoulder. "She suffered so much these past months. It broke my heart when I saw her without her hair from the chemo. Rosalyn was a wonderful, wonderful woman. Only a few weeks ago she wrote a thank-you note for the flowers we sent. Such a lady, right up to the end."

"We want you to have this," another policeman says. He hands me some Styrofoam that's been carved into a boat. They've stuck the pedals from plastic flowers all around the outside, like they do for the Rose Bowl Parade. Inside is a set of rosary beads and two toy police cars. "We thought it was appropriate. At first we thought you could put her ashes in it and let it drift out to sea, sort of as a shrine."

"I want it," Toby says, pointing at the boat. He starts to scream when I give the boat to Jared. Jared will know what to do. As a therapist, he's used to taking care of the sad details of life. He helped arrange the funeral we held last weekend, the small reception back at our house, and the luncheon we are about to have at a restaurant by the ocean in Swampscott.

"Thank you very much," I say to the retired policemen. "My mother would have been touched. You were family to her."

My mother's relationship with the Lynn Police Department began when Aunt Ella bought her a police radio after my father left us twenty years ago. I was twelve years old. The radio would help my mother get her mind off things, Aunt Ella said; hearing the troubles of others helps you forget your own. Soon my mother was listening to the radio every night after dinner, her legs pulled up on the sofa and her lap covered with an old knitted blue and white afghan that had tassels of yarn all along the top and bottom. My mother mended the afghan whenever her knees poked through. Because she worked at The Needles and Yarn Shop at the Northshore Shopping Center, she got all her thread, yarn and fabric at half price.

My mother kept a notebook next to the sofa where she'd been sleeping ever since my father left. As she listened to the radio more and more, she started filling the book with the accidents, muggings, and fires she heard about. She also kept a small folded map of Lynn in the notebook and marked the scene of any event with a little green dot.

"A two-car on Jenness, possible injuries," the voice on

the radio might say. This was the signal we were to visit the scene of a crime or accident.

Sometimes I'd be in my room looking at pictures that I'd cut out of magazines of men in bathing suits and underwear. When I heard my mother walking down the hall, I'd pull up my pajama bottoms and shove the photos under the mattress. I turned out the light, then rubbed my eyes when she came in, as if I'd just woken up.

"Where's your asthma spray?" my mother would ask. She was usually in a freshly ironed house dress. Her hair was held in place by a nearly invisible hair net. She smelled of Jean Naté and Wild Irish Rose wine.

"Right here," I said. I took the small blue canister from under my pillow where I kept it in case I had an attack in my sleep.

"Rosary beads?" my mother asked.

I hardly ever knew where they were. My father once told me all I needed to do was trust the universe to be happy, so I never saw the need to pray. I kept the beads only to avoid arguing with my mother, who never took chances and prayed regularly. In her mind, God kept score.

"You should know where the rosary beads are at all times," my mother told me. "They are as important as your asthma medicine. It's medicine for the soul."

My mother made me wipe my feet off before I got in our car, a beige Buick that she vacuumed and washed once a week. Years ago at Salem Willows, my father had won a plastic statue of the Virgin Mary that my mother glued to the dashboard. She was a careful driver (stayed five miles below the speed limit, used directionals even when leaving our driveway) and by the time we'd get to an accident, the women in pink curlers and men in sleeveless white T-shirts had already gathered, arms across their chests and their heads shaking in dismay.

We'd pull up to the scene and I'd climb on our car roof to get a better view while my mother waved hello to the policemen. I reported to my mother how many rosaries the situation warranted, from two for minor injuries to four for fatalities. Then we prayed. I kept my eyes open, taking mental notes about the condition of the injured because I knew that later on my mother would want me to go into every detail. "Incidents," as she called them, weren't over until she could explain to me exactly what had happened and why. She believed that if you found the reason for a few of these incidents, you could understand just about anything that life sent your way.

Once, after we drove to a house on Euclid Avenue to check out a man who'd had a heart attack, my mother took me to the Museum of Science in Boston to see a model of the circulatory system. She traced my finger along the major arteries to the heart, then stopped where Mr. Florentine's left ventricle had shut down.

"There," she said. "Right there is the exact spot that went wrong. That's where God made his heart stop. Any more questions?"

"Why did Dad leave us?" I asked, but she looked away.

Sometimes I listened to the radio with my mother. I imagined that my father's voice might interrupt the static to announce he was back in town. He'd vanished eight and a half months earlier for no apparent reason, leaving nothing but notes for my mother and me. I kept mine, and now and then would take it out and stare at the beautiful curve of his handwriting. I tried to copy his style. His small *r* wasn't like anyone else's I knew, and his capital letters ballooned and looped with great flourish:

> Dear Andrew,
>
> Maybe someday you will be able to understand why I had to leave. For now all I can tell you is that I am not the man any of us thought I was. I do love you and your mother very much and will be in touch.
>
> Much love to you, son.
>
> Dad

My father enclosed the names of books he loved when he was my age like *David Copperfield* and *Huckleberry Finn*. He signed the list as a doctor might sign a prescription.

Before he left us, my father bought me ice cream after church on Sundays and a new goldfish a couple of times a year. He taught me how to throw a knuckle ball. Saturday nights after hot dogs and beans, he played Rogers and Hart tunes on the piano, usually ending with my mother's favorite, "Bewitched, Bothered and Bewildered"; then the three of us would watch "Mary Tyler Moore." He worked lots of overtime in the accounting office at West Lynn Creamery to make enough for us to have a nice apartment on the good side of the city, right near the Peabody line.

A week or so after my father left, my mother took me

to a priest. Father Barrett was a heavy middle-aged man with dry, blotched skin who swiveled in his red leather chair as he spoke.

"You must help your mother in her time of need," Father Barrett said. "You must be a man."

Since I was one of the last boys in gym class to grow pubic hair, I felt Father Barrett was rushing me. I was under the impression that becoming a man would be a little more sequential, like learning math or a foreign language. Despite my reservations I told Father Barrett that I could be a man if I needed to be. I figured I'd have all my body hair by the end of school the following year; soft tufts were beginning to sprout under my arms. Adulthood might not be that far off.

"You will need another man in your life," Father Barrett went on. "That's where I can help."

"Thanks," I said, but I knew I could never talk to a man who put Vitalis in his hair and had Coke bottle glasses. My father was a thin, handsome man with red hair that swept across his head in gentle waves. His body was hard but not very muscular. His skin was white except for the spray of freckles across his shoulders. I saw him naked once, when he was changing into his bathing suit in the bathhouse at Nahant Beach. I knew at that moment exactly how I wanted to look when I got older.

"You'll need somebody to talk with about girls someday," Father Barrett said. "Someone will need to help you avoid the near occasion of sin."

"What's that?"

"Sometimes just approaching a sin can be a sin in itself," Father Barrett explained. "You need to keep away from activities like slow dancing in the dark."

Slow dancing with a girl was not on my list of "things-to-do." But "near occasion" suggested other things to me that had nothing to do with sin, like how my father would never really be in the center of my life again; the most I could hope for was that he might come close. Those words made me think about my mother, too, and the way she would get near some minor disaster without ever getting involved first-hand.

One night there was an accident on the Nahant line. A car had hit the wall that divided the lanes in the Causeway.

"Wake up, Andrew," my mother said, shaking my shoulder. She sat on the edge of my bed and told me we were driving all the way to Nahant.

"Isn't that a little out of the way?" I asked, my face in the pillow. "You don't even know any Nahant cops."

"We are needed," my mother said.

I opened my eyes to the ceiling light above me. My mother was wearing a dark dress, a sign someone might have died. Getting dressed up was a matter of respect for the dead, my mother had told me, but I assumed we had to look our best because so many people showed up for the fatal accidents. My mother handed me a shirt with a button-down collar and some khaki shorts. I grabbed my asthma spray and beads.

The air was especially warm as we drove through Lynn to the Causeway, a long man-made stretch of land that connected Lynn to Nahant. We passed the Waffle House near the beach. My father had taken us there the day he got a bonus at work. I had picked two huge waffles with chocolate sauce and whipped cream, while my mother and father shared an order of waffles and strawberries. The juke box was playing "Crocodile Rock" and my father hummed along, even though he wasn't a big Elton John fan. I loved watching my mother and father sit across from me in our blue vinyl booth and eat from the same plate. When they finished, my mother had a dab of whipped cream on the corner of her mouth. My father kissed it off with a quick kiss you might give a baby. That was the only kiss I remember him giving her. I smiled and looked around the restaurant. I wanted everyone to look our way.

As my mother and I approached the Causeway, my mother put on the radio to WEEI, the all-news station. We heard a report that a car had lost control and veered off the road into the ocean.

We left the car in the beach parking lot and walked. I saw the skid marks before we got to the accident. They started out soft and straight but soon got dark and zigzagged.

"See that?" my mother said. She pointed to a piece of rubber leaning against the low median wall. "A tire must have blown out and the driver lost control of the car. I bet he was going too fast."

I wanted to ask her how she could be so sure, but she'd already taken out the rosary beads. While my mother closed her eyes and pressed a black bead between her fingers, I took a few steps forward to see the accident better. The end of the car was sticking up from the water like the giant tail of a whale before it submerges. Two paramedics were wheeling a body on a stretcher towards the back of the ambulance. They didn't hurry. They had already given up.

I heard my father before I saw him: he screamed so loud that the crowd hushed. I watched him hold the hand of the man on the stretcher, then kiss his forehead as if he were saying good-bye. My father was drenched, his beautiful hair plastered every which way across his head, and his face glistened under the street light. When the paramedics pulled him away and shut the ambulance doors, my father started crying so hard he fell on his knees in front of everyone.

"Dad!" I yelled, but the ambulance had started to leave and nobody could hear me above the siren. My mother dropped an iron hand on my shoulder. I didn't move.

I looked at her. She was the only one I knew who might be able to console my father. When his father died, she made him chamomile tea and walked him around the house night after night until he was tired enough to go to sleep for a few hours. But now my mother couldn't do anything but stand there, pulling and twisting her beads as if she were ripping peas out of their pods.

My mother yanked me into the car. "Don't ever tell anyone what you've seen," was all she said on the way home.

My father and his lover must have been just visiting Lynn that night because the postmarks from the checks he sent my mother and me were stamped New Haven. Over the next few years the postmarks changed: Rochester, Augusta, and finally a town called Plaistow in New Hampshire. The money came every month without fail. I also got gifts in the mail at Christmas and on my birthday, usually books like *To Kill A Mockingbird* or *Johnny Tremain*, but also a ventriloquist's doll I plan to give to Toby some day.

My mother never talked to me again about what we'd seen the night of the accident. For years I followed her lead and kept quiet about my father. I tore up all my pictures of men in bathing suits, first into halves, then quarters, then, furiously, into pieces the size of confetti so my mother wouldn't find them. I didn't think she could handle knowing both my father and I loved men, and I was right. Later, when I tried to tell her about Jared, she put her wine glass down on the kitchen table and said, "I can't hear this. Go, now." I left quietly. From then on we didn't talk. We just put life's great moments like Uncle Dan's death and Toby's arrival on note cards and dropped them in the mail.

I went to visit my father in Plaistow a year or so after Jared and I adopted Toby. I loved Toby completely, even irrationally: there wasn't anything I wouldn't do for him. I needed to see if my father still had any of that fatherly love for me that I had for my new son.

"Andrew," he said simply as I stood at the door. "My God."

He was still very handsome, the touches of gray in his hair blending in with the red so that in the right light he almost looked blonde. He was wearing a white Oxford and jeans that outlined his still thin body. I wanted to touch him.

"I should have called first," I said.

"It's just such a surprise."

I'd found his address in the phone book at the library and had written to him, telling him all about Jared and me. In the letter I'd said that I wanted to see him and told him about the night at the Causeway, how I'd seen him cry over the dead man. I told him he didn't have to hide anymore, that I would help him back into the family. His reply was brief and cordial:

Dear Andrew,

In a pile of bills and junk mail, it was lovely to see your handwriting on an envelope and to hear that you are doing well. I think of you often, and continue to wish you nothing but the best in life.

Love,

Dad

My father invited me into his apartment, which I soon realized he shared: two cushy arm chairs in front of the TV, two desks, two piles of opened mail on the sideboard, one large bed in the bedroom. While my father went to make coffee, I sat and flipped through an L.L. Bean catalog from the magazine rack.

"What's his name?" I asked when he returned. He placed a tray on the coffee table between us, then sat in a blue sofa with a curved back and arms.

"Philip." My father spoke hesitantly, as if he weren't accustomed to saying his name out loud.

"The two of you have a nice place," I said, looking around for a picture of them, but I couldn't find any. "Are you happy?"

"Pretty much." He poured the coffee. "We've been together for six years. He's a teacher in the high school here. I work in the town hall in the tax department. Sometimes at lunch I walk by his classroom and see him through the window in front of all his kids."

"That sounds sweet."

"It is. We're very good for each other. What about you and—"

"Jared," I said. "We're good for each other, too. We adopted a son, you know. Jared went down to Peru for three weeks and took care of the whole thing. He came back with a three-month-old baby boy. His name is Toby."

"Congratulations. You didn't mention anything in your letter."

"I wanted to tell you in person that you were a grandfather."

My father opened his eyes wide for a split second, as if he'd been surprised by a fleeting stab of pain.

"I can't quite think of myself that way."

"I'd like Toby to get to know you."

"I don't know about that."

"Why not?"

He glanced around the room at the shelves of alphabetized books, the table by the window with the perfectly arranged irises, the shoes lined up against the wall on the mat by the door.

"I guess it just sounds too disruptive."

"You've taught me all I need to know about disruption already," I said. It slipped out.

My father sighed. He rubbed his fingers against his clenched lips. When he looked at me, his face was as pained as I ever remembered it.

"I'm sorry," he said. "I had every intention of calling you, even asking to see you once I settled down. But the more time went by, the harder it got to pop into your life again. All I had to do was blink and a few more years were gone."

I turned to the window and watched a car go by. An ice cream truck pulled up to the curb. Soon three or four children in shorts and T-shirts gathered around the counter. Suddenly I missed Toby terribly, and needed to feel him wriggle in my arms. I couldn't understand how my father found it easier to stay away.

"I hated you for leaving," I said, still looking outside. "For a long time I couldn't help but hate who I was, too. I used to think all I needed was to know someone who was like me to feel OK. But that someone ended up being you. It only made it worse because of what you'd done to Mom and me."

"I'm very sorry. What more can I—"

"No. Please listen to me," I said. "I used to lie awake in bed wondering if you were one of those older men who had sex with other men in the woods along the highway because they couldn't get it anywhere else. Then I'd get scared I'd end up that way. I'd read in the paper about these guys who were arrested by state troopers. They published all their names. I was afraid I'd see you listed someday."

"You didn't want people to know about me," my father said. "I don't blame you. That's one of the reasons I left the way I did."

"Maybe it's time you came back."

"But why?" my father asked. "You've got a good life as it is. You and Jared can have a child and do whatever you want to do. I envy you. If things were like this twenty years ago I wouldn't have had to leave. But now I'm used to living a certain way."

"We can change that," I said.

"I doubt it. Philip and I love each other, but we lead very private lives." He splayed his fingers and waved them in front of me. "No rings. To most people Philip's just my friend. If I came back into your life, you'd want your son to know, and his friends, and Ella. Everybody. I'm not sure I could handle that. I can't live like you after being silent for so long."

"So there's nowhere to go with this?"

"I guess not." My father sat and reached across the coffee table. He squeezed my hand.

"Fuck this," I whispered. I pulled away and put my arm across my face so he wouldn't see my eyes filling up.

My father got up from the sofa and knelt beside me, patting my knee. "I'm sorry. I've hurt you again. I'm not good for you."

"You have to be good for me," I said. "You're my father. You don't have a choice."

"OK," he said softly. "Maybe we can talk again. But think about it first. The only way this can work for me is if I can be who I am. And that means being quiet."

"I keep quiet about you now."

"It's easier when I'm not around," he said. "Take a few weeks. Then call if you'd like."

I didn't call. When I understood my father and I would never really share our lives, I didn't know what was left for the two of us to salvage.

But I tried once more, when my mother died. I left a message on his answering machine asking him to come down for the service with Philip. I invited him to stay with Jared and Toby and me. He sent me a sympathy card a few days later, with this brief note:

My dear Andrew,

Although I am not able to attend
the service for your mother, please
know that I am deeply moved by her
passing. I loved her very much, just as
I have always loved you. My blessings
to you, Jared and Toby.

Dad

I touch his card now in the inside pocket of my sports
coat after I've scattered my mother's ashes and changed out
of my wet clothes. We've arrived at the restaurant with its
huge windows overlooking the ocean, ordered and received
our lunch, and are listening to Father Barrett begin grace.
Aunt Ella insisted we invite him, and as he blesses our food,
I wonder if having a priest at the service was a good idea.
The accident on the Causeway didn't keep my mother from
listening to the police radio every night, but her heart really
wasn't in it. She stopped trying to explain to me why a car
went through a red light on Maple Street, or what exactly
caused a stroke. She'd lost faith and said her prayers like
you recite the alphabet or the Pledge of Allegiance. By the
time I left home, we'd even stopped going to church. As
Father Barrett says "Amen" and we all lift our heads, I wonder if this was what she would have wanted.

"You OK?" Jared asks when we sit down.

"Yup," I say with a sigh. "Not really. We can talk later."

"I've always said you could judge a man's commitment
by the life expectancy of pets he keeps," Aunt Ella says to

me from across the table. "A man with a hamster will give you two years. Marry a man with a parrot and you've got him for life. Your father didn't even own a pet when he met Rosalyn, so I can't say I was surprised."

"But they were good to each other," I manage to say. Jared puts his hand on my leg under the table.

"Of course they were," Aunt Ella says as she looks at one of the cops from the corner of her eye as if to say *We'll just let him think that for now.*

"They were," I say again, this time more firmly. Jared and I are the only ones at the table who know why my father really left. I don't want anyone to think that he beat her or left in a drunken rage.

Aunt Ella stands and lifts her glass of wine in a toast to my mother. She talks about her as if she really knew her, and she did, of course, back when my mother was full of hope, before she discovered, as I did, that knowing why something has happened doesn't always make it less painful.

Jared gives Toby a small glass of ginger ale to toast with, and we all clink our glasses to my mother's life.

"I wish my father were here," I whisper to Jared. "I want to call him. I'll be right back."

I find the pay phone and take his number out of my wallet. I have no idea what I'll say. Maybe I want to hear him tell me he's thinking of me the day I've memorialized my mother, that he's with me in spirit even though he couldn't come down from Plaistow. The phone rings three times before my father picks up. I hear his gentle hello. My neck pounds. My face gets warm. I don't even greet him. I slowly hang up. I run into the men's room and lean against the wall, trying to breathe normally again. I began the day burying one parent and am ending it burying another.

I splash cold water on my face and dab my eyes with my handkerchief so they're only a little red when I return to the table. The guests are passing around their plates of fried scallops, clams, and shrimp, as if they were eating in a boarding house. Aunt Ella sways to Sinatra's "Nice 'n' Easy," which plays low in the background. Toby kneels on his chair, sipping milk from a straw. I sit between him and Jared, who smiles as he fills my glass with water. He hands me the basket of warm bread.

"Did you talk to him?" he asks.

"Almost," I say, and take his hand in mine.

PLUNGE

"*I*'m going to start doing massages for pets," Veronica said. "A career might help me get my life on track."

"I'd love to talk about this, but now's not a good time," I said. Veronica was too preoccupied to realize that Theo, my boyfriend, hadn't shown up for our commitment ceremony yet. She had just found her date making out behind the sculptured hedges with one of the women who was supposed to be tending bar.

"I can't believe he did this to me. That sonofabitch," Veronica said.

"Hey, I'm on edge too. I'm petrified Theo isn't going to show. Where the hell is he?" I was still holding tight to the possibility he might have taken a wrong turn on his way here. We'd rented a mansion in Waltham for the wedding, and he'd only been here once, the day we visited and turned in the deposit.

"I'm sorry, Peter," Veronica said. "I should be more sensitive. It's just that even when you're frazzled you seem so together. How could I tell? Theo'll be here, I know he will. You're looking very handsome, you know that, don't you?" She reached out to straighten my glasses. Veronica was the only woman I knew who could see eye to eye with me without standing on her toes.

Sal DiFillipo came up behind Veronica and gave me a little wave over her shoulder. He was tall and thin and had dyed his hair blonde. His dark roots still showed; I assumed that was in vogue these days with the twenty-something crowd. He was one of a few people I'd invited from Mt. Auburn Country Day, the school where I'd taught English for the past twenty-one years.

"I'm all ready," Sal said. He pulled a folded sheet of paper from his checkered sports coat. He and Veronica were to speak at the ceremony. "So, how's the groom?"

"I can't find him," I said.

"I meant you."

"Nervous as hell. People are going to start to notice he's not here."

"Well just relax. The whole affair is going to be fabulous."

"Do you think so?" I asked. I hated it when I let my insecurities show. But what the hell was I getting myself into? Theo and I weren't even married yet and he'd already left me. Or maybe not. Maybe he'd had a very minor accident. A few bumps and bruises, no broken bones. But if it wasn't serious, couldn't he have used the car phone to let me know what was going on? I looked at Sal. He could get a smile out of me even during faculty meetings. "Make me feel better. Please, Sal."

"Honey, people haven't stop talking about this shindig since they got here," he said. "Of course, none of it's positive. Now, if you'll excuse me, I'm going to talk to that adorable librarian over there."

"There he is," Veronica said.

"Thank God. Where?"

"Not Theo," Veronica said. "I mean the asshole." She began puffing her cigarette double time. I followed her eyes to the guy she'd brought to the wedding. She tended to fall for this type of man: tweedy, bearded, scraggly hair. What you might get at Central Casting if you asked for a therapist. Veronica was crushed when he told her he was actually a big fruit and vegetable man for Star Market.

"Why do you go out with these guys, Veronica?" I asked.

"My therapist says it's because my mother constantly threatened to kill herself when I was growing up. That surprised me. I thought all mothers talked about killing themselves."

Next to Theo, Veronica was my closest friend. She'd stuck by me through everything from the divorce from my ex-wife to the string of horrible love affairs afterwards.

"You'll be OK," I said.

"So will you," she said. "Oh, fuck it. I mean, what the hell is Valium for, right?" She reached into her bag and dumped some tiny orange pills into her hand. When a waiter went by with a tray of champagne, she grabbed a glass, gulped the pills down, then put the glass back.

"Veronica, those are sedatives, not tic-tacs," I said.

"Don't worry. A few little pills won't hurt me. I've got to get my mind off this guy."

"You can start by helping me find my husband. Call

everyone Theo knows."

"Everyone he knows is here."

"Then check some of the places he hangs out. Just find out where he is." I kissed her on the cheek. "Love you."

I went the guitarist to stall for time. Most of the guests were still in their little circles, chatting about the guests in the little circles behind them. A few had begun to look around for something to happen. When they saw me I just smiled as confidently as I could, but I felt like the Social Director on the *Titanic*.

The guitarist gave me his hand. "Congratulations," he said.

"Can you play a few more?" I asked him. "We can't find Theo anywhere. We've got to stall."

"I'll play as long as you'd like."

Stephen, the minister who'd agreed to marry us, wheeled himself next to me. I'd grown up with him in Beverly. He'd had a stroke about two months before the wedding and had lost most of his feeling on his left side. Before then, he was a solid man in his forties with thick black hair and slightly pock-marked skin. He must have lost twenty-five pounds lying in his bed in the rehab center. I wasn't sure if he'd aged fifteen years since the stroke or whether I'd convinced myself he looked older so I wouldn't have to face the fact that someone else so close to my own age had taken ill so suddenly. I was used to drawn-out hospital scenes from AIDS. I'd forgotten there were other things that hit you without warning.

"Don't you love my necklace?" Stephen asked. Veronica, Sal and I had to sneak him out of the rehab earlier in the day. We threw a long string of fake pearls around him once we got him off the hospital grounds.

"What am I going to do, Stephen?" I asked. "We're going to have to bring you back soon before they send out a warrant for my arrest."

"You know Theo. I bet he's just putting that last bit of gel in his hair."

"I hope you're right. You don't think he's having cold feet, do you?"

"Theo? He's been waiting for this day all his life. He's not going anywhere."

"I wish I believed you."

"Maybe it's your own cold feet you're worried about."

"No way," I lied. "My feet are as warm as toast."

Stephen was sleeping when we came into his room the morning of the wedding, so I sat down and browsed through the stack of get well cards while Sal stood and looked around the room as if he were taking mental notes as to how to spruce the place up. Veronica read the personals in the *Phoenix* with a thick yellow highlighter in her hand.

"But you've got a date for the wedding," I said to her. "Maybe something will come of that."

"You can never have too many opportunities," Veronica said. "It's sort of like using two forms of birth control. You never know when one's going to bail out on you."

I stroked Stephen's hand to gently wake him.

"Morning, sunshine," I said.

"Hey," Stephen said. "Isn't this the big day? What are you doing here?"

"Just a little prenuptial visit."

A nurse walked in and stood at the door. "You guys only have half an hour," she said. "Don't make me come back and ask you to leave. Just be adults and do as you're told."

"Where did she get her training, Alcatraz?" Sal asked after the nurse left the room. He pulled at the curtain that hung at the head of the bed. "This is a disgrace. Who decorates this place, anyway? And look at your hair Stevie. You can't even think about moving those limbs of yours until you get yourself a good stylist. Have you no priorities?" Stephen had undergone surgery shortly after he was rushed to the Medical Center in Boston. They had shaved his head, and his hair was coming in bristly and uneven.

"I'm supposed to get a haircut next week," Stephen said.

"Don't let them touch you!" Sal screamed. "Really, love, you wouldn't let some Newbury Street salon queen work on your brain, would you? Then do not let some cranium queen touch your hair."

Stephen laughed, then turned to me. "Well, good luck today," he said. "I wish I could be there. I want lots of pictures of the grooms. Where is Theo, anyway?"

"Bad luck for the groom to see the groom the day of the wedding," I said. I looked to Sal for a signal to present our plan to sneak Stephen out for the ceremony, but he was peering over Veronica's shoulder. We'd decided to wait until the last minute to see how Stephen felt. His health varied greatly from one day to another; we didn't want to get his hopes up, only to find out he was just too weak to leave. A friend of mine who taught religion at Mt. Auburn said she would do the ceremony for us in a pinch.

"Here's one," Veronica said. She took the cap off her

highlighter. "White male, blond hair, blue eyes, swimmer's build, great body, looking for similar woman."

"Why doesn't he just go out with a full-length mirror?" Stephen said.

"Now, now," Sal said. "He's deeper than that. Look. It says 'relationship first.'"

"Which means you have to have dinner with him before you go to bed," I said.

"O ye of little faith," Sal said.

"If you want something to last for more than a few hours," Stephen said, "you'll have to have more in common than hair color."

"So do you really think Theo and I will last?" I asked Stephen.

"What are you talking about?" Stephen said. "Of course you will."

"Do I hear second thoughts?" Veronica asked from her newspaper.

"No. I just keep thinking of everything that could go wrong, like our age difference. Christ, I'm ten years older than he is. He could have been a student of mine."

I'd already highlighted my hair twice since the two of us met, I went to the gym four instead of three times a week now, and I covered my face with Retin-A every night. I didn't even know how I should introduce Theo anymore. Lover? Partner? Husband? Theo loved to tell the story of the woman at work who looked at my picture on his desk and thought I was his father. That sealed it for me. I really was too old for him. Only we wouldn't face it until I was in my late fifties, when Theo no longer found me attractive.

"You aren't that much older than Theo," Stephen said.

"The average age difference between gay men in long-term relationships is seven years." He knew every statistic imaginable about being gay. He'd had a boyfriend once, but only for a month or so. Everything else he knew came from books.

Sal and I winked at each other for the go-ahead.

"So, how badly do you want to leave this place?" Sal asked.

"Don't be cruel," Stephen said. "You know how badly."

"Well, Stevie," Sal said. "I've been casing this joint since you checked in. I know all the ropes. It just so happens that Nurse Diesel is off duty at twelve when that sweet little Roger comes on. I think we can get you out of here in a snap and back by three."

"We want you to marry us," I said. "We've got it all planned."

"We're going to get you out of here before the bigwigs find out," Veronica said.

"Bigwigs?" Sal said. "In this place? Only toupees."

Veronica grabbed Stephen's clothes while Sal and I hoisted him up from the bed and into his chair.

"Now look casual," I said as we left the room. Saturday morning cartoons on Nickelodeon blared from the rooms into the hallway.

"Where are you going?" Nurse Roger asked when we passed the desk.

"The solarium," Sal said. "Back in a jiffy. Ta-ta."

Sal pushed Stephen with such an air of confidence that Nurse Roger didn't give another look.

"Breaks my heart, doing that to Rog," Sal said. "If anyone finds out, it'll be his buns in a sling."

"You are all amazing," Stephen said when we got to the

car. "What would I do without you?"

"Sometimes I think I could be very happy just living with the three of you," I said. "Who needs hot, passionate love, anyway?"

"Look, Peter, if you're nervous about going through with the ceremony for yourself, do it for me. I'd kill to be hitching up with the M.O.M.D." M.O.M.D. was Veronica-speak for Man of My Dreams. It's what she even called me sometimes.

Man of My Dreams. Is that what Theo was?

*A*t the wedding, the guitarist was getting into the spirit of stalling for time, although his choice of songs (he was now playing the opening riff of "Stairway to Heaven") made me question his gay credentials. I was glad we'd hired a DJ for dancing after the ceremony who'd promised to stock up on Motown for us. Just as the guitarist got to the melody, Veronica came running out of the house.

"M.O.M.D. found," she said.

"What's the problem?" I asked.

"The problem is he's in the Jacuzzi at Dave's Gym."

"Doesn't he know what time it is?"

"Oh, he knows all right. He just refuses to get out. You'd better go talk to him."

So I drove to Dave's, checking the rearview mirror periodically to make sure my hair was in place and my bow tie wasn't crooked. I always tried to look my best going to Dave's. Sal once advised me to shower before working out at a gay gym; it was the only way to look really fabulous.

I didn't know exactly what I was going to say to Theo,

whether I would beg for him to come to the ceremony or tell him a la Gershwin that I was calling the whole thing off. I imagined singing the words to him in my tuxedo, then nearly cringed in panic thinking of sleeping in an empty bed. Nobody held me like Theo at night.

"Theo!" I said. I had to speak above the hum of the Jacuzzi filter and "It's Raining Men," the song they played at least every other hour at Dave's.

Theo slipped underwater until he disappeared beneath the foam, then he resurfaced. He wasn't the sexiest man alive when he was naked, but he was sexy enough for me. He still had a good ten pounds or so he needed to shed. We went to the gym two or three times a week, but Theo spent most of his time in the Jacuzzi or at the juice bar.

"Would you please tell me what's going on?" I asked.

"I'm just relaxing," Theo said. "Would you like a drink?"

Theo had brought a few plastic cups from the bar into the Jacuzzi. They were lined up along the edge of the tub.

"What I'd like is an explanation," I said.

"Why don't you just come in and sit next to me?"

"We've got a yard full of guests waiting for you!"

"They'll be OK. Get in here."

I didn't know what I really expected to happen, but I'd reached the point when doing anything seemed better than doing nothing at all, so I got into the water. One of the things I love about Theo is that he can get me to do things I wouldn't dare do if I used my brain for half a minute. I looked around. The locker room was empty except for a guy in the shower. I'd forgotten Dave's was usually empty on Saturdays in the summer. I untied my shoes, then carefully took off my tuxedo and hung it piece by piece on the pegs on the wall. When I was naked, I stuck my toe in the water and slowly made my way down the steps to get used to the temperature. Finally I let my whole body drop into the tub.

"Christ, this is hot," I said.

"You'll get used to it," Theo said. "It just takes awhile. Then you'll never want to get out."

"So what's going on?"

The man who had been in the shower stepped up to the Jacuzzi with *The New York Times* tucked under his arm. He dropped his towel and entered the water. He smiled at us, then delicately walked over our legs and sat in the corner of he tub.

"Glad to have you," Theo said as if a guest he'd invited to a pool party had arrived. I was marrying Martha Stewart.

"Well?" I asked.

"I know you're upset," Theo said. "Just give me some time and I can explain the whole thing."

"We haven't got any time, Theo!"

"There you are!" This was from Stephen, whom Sal was wheeling in.

"What's your excuse?" Veronica yelled in tow. She walked into the locker room and to the Jacuzzi area, her hand across her eyes.

"You guys, please," I said. "Could you just give us a few minutes? We need to straighten a few things out, that's all."

"Anyone have something to write with?" the man with *The New York Times* said. "I want to do the crossword puzzle."

Sal produced a pen. He and Veronica and Stephen looked at me as if they expected me to do something. I felt like some bad act at the aquarium, an untalented performing seal who hadn't even learned how to balance a ball on his nose so just splashed around instead. I tried to ignore our little audience.

"So," I said to Theo. "Is this it?"

"What's a four-letter word meaning *fluctuate* ?" The *New York Times* man asked.

"Try *bend*," Sal said.

"No, it has to have an *a* in it."

"What about *wave*?"

"Doesn't work. The *a* is the third letter."

"*Sway*."

"That's it!" the man said. "Hey, you're good with words."

"Thanks," Sal said with a smile.

"I'm Rob."

"Sal DiFillipo."

"Why don't you come in and join me?"

Sal stripped down and went into the water.

"Boys, you've got a decision to make," Veronica said. "We can't wait here all day. I've got a date tonight."

"Really?" Stephen asked.

"Well, not a date, date," Veronica said. "It's more like a possible pre-date telephone conversation, if you know what I mean. I'm talking with someone who might help me with that new business I want to open."

"What business is that?" Stephen asked. He moved back a little in his wheelchair.

"Pet massage."

"Hey, that's what I do," Rob said.

"You're kidding," Veronica said.

"I've been doing it for ten years. Only been bitten once." He stood and turned so his backside was facing Veronica.

"Right here," he said, pointing to his left cheek.

"Ah, shit," Veronica said. "I thought I'd be starting something original." She looked like she was about to cry.

"Better hop in, my dear," Sal said. "Join the tub of lost souls."

"Oh, what the fuck," Veronica said. "Everyone here is gay, right?"

"As gay as geese," Rob said, his arm now around Sal.

"OK folks," Sal said. "Somebody better give somebody a ring here or we're walking."

"Well, at least some of us are," Stephen said.

Sal started singing "Standing at the Crossroads of Love." He was a great Supremes fan.

"Theo?" I asked.

Theo said nothing.

"Good-bye, then," I said. I stood and grabbed a towel. I took my tux off the hook and headed towards the lockers.

"Wait a minute," Theo called. He got out of the water, wrapped himself, then ran to me. He pulled me into the sauna where the rocks in the stove crackled. I put a towel on the bench so as not to burn myself.

"If we're going to have any chance at all, you've got to talk to me," I said. "What's wrong?"

"Pimple," Theo mumbled.

"Say that again?"

"I have a pimple."

"You have a pimple."

Aha.

"And this pimple is somehow related to why you didn't show up today?"

"It isn't just any old pimple. I have a pimple the size of

a dinner plate right here on my chin." Theo thrust his head my way so I could see what he was talking about.

"I don't see a thing," I said. "And I don't believe that's what's bothering you."

"I did show up, you know," Theo said. "I stood at the gate and watched all the people milling about. I watched your sister and her husband bicker back and forth and watched Veronica try to have a good time with that awful man she brought with her. And then I thought, Why are we doing this? This is what our straight friends do to make themselves miserable. We should be making our own rules."

"What kind of rules do you want to make?"

"I don't know. That's why I took off to soak in the Jacuzzi. To decide exactly what I wanted for us. Haven't you been doing any thinking yourself?"

"I'm a teacher, remember? I play by the rules, even when they scare me."

I'd begun to think it was my innate conformity that made me bring up the possibility of the ceremony in the first place. Maybe we should have just agreed to keep living with each other and not complicate matters by formally committing. But wasn't it all simply a matter of perception? These were new rules, I told myself; this wasn't like my heterosexual marriage. There were no papers to sign, no blood test to take, no Catholic priest at the altar.

"If you think about it, it's not legally binding," I said. "Does that help?"

"That's a good thing to remember," Theo said. "We can get out of this pretty easily if it doesn't work out."

I didn't like hearing Theo speak in quite those terms, but I closed my eyes and remained calm as he continued.

"And if one night twelve years from now you happen to be at some convention and meet this heartbreaker who's willing to go to bed with you just once, well, then, technically, it's not adultery," Theo said.

I gulped. "Would you really go to bed with him?" I managed to say.

"I said *if*, Peter. Don't put words in my mouth."

"Well, I wouldn't go to bed with him," I said.

"Neither would I," Theo said. "But knowing that I have the option is sort of a life raft."

I wiped a bead of sweat off Theo's nose.

"How's that pimple doing?" I asked.

"Maybe it isn't so big," Theo said. "Maybe they won't be staring at it so much."

"Maybe the guests don't have to be there when we tie the knot. Would that make things any less pressured for you if we did it right now?"

"I think it might," Theo said. He kissed me on the lips. "I love you very much. I'm ready."

I followed Theo back to the Jacuzzi. He had a spring in his step.

"Will you marry us, Stephen?" Theo asked. "Here and now?"

"I'd be honored."

"Better come on in, Reverend," Sal said.

I helped Stephen off with his pants, got him out of the chair, and took off his shirt. Veronica held his hand as he slid into the water. Then Theo and I plunged in, too.

Theo wrapped his arm around me.

"This is a first," Stephen said. "I don't know where to start."

"Better keep it short," I said. "We don't have much time."

"Forget about the time, Peter," Theo said. "Don't worry about a thing."

I really wanted to forget. I wanted to stop worrying that I might not know Theo well enough to marry him, and that he might actually spend the night with that hypothetical young hunk at a convention in another ten years, despite what he said in the sauna, and despite the fact that Theo worked as a secretary and had never been to a convention in his life.

I turned to Stephen, who was moving his good arm in the water, splashing like a child. He let his whole body float: one leg at a time, then his other arm. He dropped his head back and let that float, too.

"I'm weightless," Stephen said, laughing.

I put my head on Theo's shoulder and wondered if we would ever feel as light.

MOTHER COUNTRY

"Will you look at this wall?" Cecily says, her head in the guidebook. "It goes all around Avila."

She sits across from my lover and me at a restaurant called El Museo del Jamón near the Plaza Mayor in Madrid. The Museum of Ham? How could we just walk by? The menu lured us in, too: three-course specials for 900 pesetas including mineral water or wine. Long shanks of ham hang from the ceiling over the bar, deep red and purple, the color of a bruise.

"What do you say, Nick?" Cecily flattens the book and pushes it in front of me. She wears a thin gold bracelet, a gift from Ignacio and me. "Are you coming or not?"

I sigh. "Oh, I guess."

"Great," Cecily says. She flips the sunglasses down from her head, then looks around for the waiter.

"But you've got to get some food in you, Cecily," Ignacio says.

"You expect me to eat this?" On the white plate in front of her is a grayish-blue fish with its tail stuck in its mouth.

"It looks like it tried to devour itself," I say. "A Kamikaze trout."

"That's impossible," Ignacio says. "It would die before it finished the first bite."

"You guys aren't making it any more appetizing to me."

"You're not going to eat it anyway," I say.

We continue to bicker like children in this city filled with children. We do our best to ignore them, but they are everywhere, even running around the neighborhood bars, blithely oblivious to our loss. Yesterday, when three or four girls got on our subway car to sell tiny packs of Kleenex, Cecily buried her head in her hands to keep from crying. Ignacio sat beside her and rubbed her back. There's nothing left for anyone to say.

Ignacio fills our glasses with the last of the red wine. "My favorite food group," he says. "I consider wine a fruit."

"I consider myself one, too," I say.

Ignacio laughs as he brings the glass to his lips. He has a smooth, round face, and a round figure to match.

"*Café?*" the waiter asks. I look at Ignacio and Cecily. The train for Avila leaves at two. Do we have enough time? "*Joven?*" the waiter says to me.

"He just called you a young man," Ignacio says. He takes his last bite of chicken cooked in garlic and oil. I'm the only one who ordered ham.

I smile. "I can't remember the last time someone called me young. Not with these strands of gray." I pull down a lock of hair between my eyes.

"It distinguishes you," Ignacio says.

"From younger men," I say.

"The train station is fifteen minutes on the metro." Cecily says *metro* instead of *subway* now that she's been in Madrid for five days.

"We should leave, then," Ignacio says. He sends the waiter off for our check.

Cecily looks once more at the picture of Avila before she returns the guidebook to her canvas bag. "I want to climb one of the watchtowers and look down on the entire city inside the wall."

"I brought extra film," Ignacio says.

"You're such a boy scout," I say. I saw him pack bottled water for all of us, bandages, playing cards for the train ride, and a small roll of the Tía María cookies we've grown to like here.

"It must feel so safe to live there," Cecily says. "So sheltered."

"Can't we just go back and have a siesta?" I ask.

"You know, Nick, you are allowed to have fun on this trip," Ignacio says.

"Not fun," I say. "*Simulated* fun. This entire trip is a Simulated Fun Activity. A classic SFA."

How can we have real fun? How can we forget the baby has died?

*I*gnacio is Mexican by birth, but he has lived in Boston since he came to the BU School of Social Work ten years ago.

"I've always wanted to visit the land of my great-great-grandparents," he said to Cecily and me one night. Cecily was two months pregnant. "How about Spain next summer?

The three of us and our new child in the mother country."

But the baby was born early, and was put in neonatal intensive care with heart problems.

"A valve isn't pumping the right way," the doctor said. "There's leakage. We'd like to do the surgery as soon as possible."

"Who is that man?" I said after the doctor left the room. "He knows me well enough to tell me where the men's room is or when visiting hours are over. He has no right to talk to me about leaking hearts."

"She'll be OK. I can feel it in my bones," Cecily said from her hospital bed. Ignacio held her hand.

"Shit, this is going to be bad," I said. "That's what my bones say."

"I can't have this conversation, Nick," Cecily said. "We need positive energy right now. They'll take care of her here. We couldn't be in a better place."

But in the end there wasn't even enough time left for the doctor to say one of those doctorly things like we'll take this one step at a time. The baby died that night.

To fill our time, we started the first of our Simulated Fun Activities: watching award shows at Cecily's. Not just the biggies like the Oscars and the Grammys, but also the People's Choice and the Country Music Awards. Cecily's already talked about a Miss America evening in September.

"I want a diploma for going through this," I told Ignacio and Cecily on the way to the funeral. I wanted to clutch it for a while, then hang it on a wall, then pack it up in storage so I could forget about it with all our junk.

"I don't want a diploma," Cecily said. "I want my mother. I've never really missed her until now."

Cecily's love life has been straight out of Ann Landers: affairs with married, middle-aged men from the suburbs with a son or a daughter in high school. There's usually a month of bliss, followed by confusion. Then comes the letter from him, the threats to tell all from her, and a final farewell drink at the Lenox Hotel bar. She calls Ignacio, who arrives with a feel-good novel and flowers. It's a role he's played for many years, ever since we moved into our apartment on Mass Ave and met Cecily, our new neighbor, two floors above.

For age reasons, health-of-the-baby reasons, and odds-against-ever-finding-a-husband-as-she-neared-forty reasons, Cecily set thirty-five as the last year she would spend childless. A few days after her birthday, she brought up the idea of co-parenting to Ignacio, who popped the question to me.

"The baby would stay with Cecily," Ignacio said. "We'd be the fathers. Both of us."

Ignacio and I had talked about adopting, but we'd never considered Cecily being the mother. "I'm not sure I'd feel very fatherly with the baby somewhere else," I said.

"It makes the most sense. She's got the time and an extra room." Cecily usually worked out of her apartment. An inheritance from her father had allowed her to support herself while she wrote her first novel and articles for the *Phoenix* .

"What if we say no?" I asked.

"She'll just go to a sperm bank. We're going to have a baby in our lives either way."

"It just doesn't feel right."

"Nothing ever feels right to you at first," Ignacio said. "Soon as Cecily's pregnant you'll forget you ever had doubts."

"This isn't like the time you got me to try sushi. This is

a baby we're talking about."

"I know," Ignacio said softly, unable to keep from smiling. "A baby. Imagine."

His eyes started to well up, and I couldn't say no.

Two months later, Ignacio went to donate his sperm at the health center. He got nervous, and the nurse only had *Playboy* and *Penthouse* to arouse him.

"I couldn't perform," he told Cecily and me when he got home. "It's a wedding night nightmare come true."

"We'll go with you next time for moral support," Cecily said.

"We'll sneak in a copy of *Advocate Men*," I said. "But if you can't do it, you can't do it. It's no big deal. You already have about a trillion children."

Ignacio mails monthly checks to Save the Children, UNICEF, and a bunch of other child support agencies that send him black and white photos of poor kids and their report cards. I tell our friends he has Sally Struthers' beeper number.

The following week, the nurse at the clinic again offered Ignacio a selection of hetero porn.

"Got my own," he said, pointing to his backpack. He winked at me.

"Don't have too much fun in there," I whispered to him. "You're still a married man."

While Ignacio was in Room 2, Cecily sat on the sofa leafing through an old *People*. I paced.

"You're not going to become a father *today*, Nick," Cecily said. She handed me a stick of Dentyne. "Chew this and calm down."

Ignacio was smiling and flushed when he came out of

the room. He gave us a high five and pulled three Cuban cigars out of his backpack.

"You think of everything," Cecily said.

"Ignacio, darling, you'll make our child a wonderful mother," I said in my campiest voice.

After four more trips to the clinic, we finally had enough sperm to inseminate Cecily on a Friday night in July. Ignacio arranged vases of pink and white teacup roses on the edge of the bathtub and lined lilac-scented votive candles around the sink. On a tray he placed what we called the turkey baster for the insemination, along with two thin mints.

"Ready for conception, my love?" he said to Cecily. Her sandy hair touched the shoulders of her turquoise, black and white silk kimono. The robe was slightly open below her neck, revealing a spray of light freckles.

"I'm ready," Cecily said.

"One more thing." Ignacio reached into the pocket of the white smoking jacket he'd found at Goodwill for the occasion and produced a black velvet box done up in silver ribbon. "For you. From us. To celebrate our baby-to-be."

Cecily giggled when she unwrapped the box. "Tiffany's. Wow." She slipped the bracelet on her left wrist. It was called a "Kisses" bracelet: an 18k gold chain of "x's."

Ignacio bowed his head and waved Cecily into the bathroom with great flourish. Cecily blew a kiss before she shut the bathroom door.

"We're with you," Ignacio said.

He joined me in the living room where the two of us drank champagne.

"I feel so useless," I said. "Like a guest at this holiday meal the two of you have invited me to. I keep wondering when it's time for me to leave. Isn't there anything I can do?"

"Sure there is," Ignacio said. He kissed me on the cheek, then went to the stereo. He put on "Take A Look At Me Now" by Phil Collins, the song we danced to the night we met at Buddies. He lifted me off the sofa, took me in his arms, and slow danced as he stroked my hair.

"You really will be a father with me," Ignacio said.

"But what do I know about babies? I crunch numbers for a living, remember? What do I *do*, Ignacio?"

"Trust me."

I did. Ignacio brought home books that I read cover to cover: *The Expectant Father, The Expectant Mother, How to Raise a Non- Racist Child.* I took notes on Brazleton, Leach, and Spock. I looked forward to our Lamaze classes and helping Cecily with her breathing patterns. The three of us watched videos. I learned all the stats about the APGAR test, average weight at birth, heart rates and body temps. Gradually all those numbers added up to one child in my mind, our child.

We board the train at the Atrocha Station, squeezing our way past large elderly women dressed in black and grubby looking students with overstuffed backpacks. Hiking boots dangle from the frames; sleeping bags are rolled up and tied to the bottoms. A group of kids hover over a beat up copy of *Let's Go: Spain. I* think about what similar guides for my life might be called, a series of *Let's Forget* books. *Let's Forget: Children's Hospital. Let's Forget: Leaking Hearts. Let's Forget: Babies.*

Cecily and Ignacio sit next to each other on the train so they can play cards. A student leans against the arm of a seat and strums his guitar. In front of me sit a darkly handsome mother and father and their three boys. The children look like yodelers in matching green shorts with attached bibs and straps that crisscross in the back.

"Holá," says the middle boy, about four years old. He is on his knees, looking over his seat.

"Holá," I say, then begin reading my European edition of *Time*.

"Do you speak English?" asks the father. He is standing with the baby yodeler in his arms.

"Yes, I do," I say. "I'm from the United States."

"I understand," he says. "I study English, but not much. But I like to practice when I am able."

I smile and resume the article on the Asian market plunge.

"What part of the United States do you come from?" the man asks. He's speaking Berlitz English, and I half expect him to repeat the copyright warning he's heard over and over at the beginning of his tape.

"I'm from Boston."

"Do you have some children?"

Surely he's skipped a few questions. What about *What do you do for a living?* or *Do you like the scenery in Spain?*

"Do you see any children?" I ask him.

We stand in the aisle as the backpacks, bags of bread and fruit, guitar cases, and the yodeler's diaper bag are taken off the racks above the seats. The air in the train is hot and sticky. I can smell the faint aroma of pot that has seeped into the denim the backpackers wear.

We're the last to step off the train into the group of travelers milling about outside the station. Ignacio squirts some sun block into his hands, then rubs it on my arms. He does the same for himself and Cecily. From his backpack he pulls out a blue cap with a yellow bear—Madrid's logo—on the front.

"This'll protect your eyes from the sun," he says to me. "I've brought an extra."

"God, it's sweltering," I say.

"Just don't think hot and you'll feel better," Cecily says.

"My brain is not a thermostat."

"To cool you off," Ignacio says. He takes out a bottle of Crespa mineral water, squats down and pours into three paper cups he's packed. When he offers us cookies, Cecily declines.

We are on the outside of the city. Every two hundred feet or so a watchtower sticks out of the wall. The wall and the towers are the same height and made of the same large, sun-bleached rocks. It looks like an enormous roll of corrugated cardboard has been stretched around Avila. Here and there clumps of green branches hang over the towers. They could be nests.

By the time we finish our water, other tourists have taken the few taxis available to ride to the city's gate or have gone inside the train station bar for their *merienda*. Suddenly, Avila seems harsh and empty.

"Let's get going," Ignacio says as he gathers the paper cups for the trash. "I want to make it to the cathedral before it closes."

He leads us to the road that runs parallel to the wall in the distance. Cecily walks beside him while I fall a few steps behind. They both stop when she fans herself with her large-brimmed sun hat.

"See," I say, "It really *is* hot, no matter what you're thinking."

"Thank you, Mr. Reality Check," Cecily says. "I'm glad you—"

She is interrupted by a strange clicking sound. I turn to see two women in long black skirts swoop down from the side of the hill. Over their shoulders they carry piles of pastel lace that contrast with their dark clothes and hair. I expect to see castanets but realize that one of them is clicking her tongue against the roof of her mouth.

"Look!" says the larger of the two women, whose skirt bunches tight around her wide waist. She runs a shawl through her hands to get Cecily's attention.

"Shawls made by hand," her companion says. She looks younger until she opens her mouth to reveal she is missing some front teeth. Her eyes are fixed on Cecily's Tiffany bracelet.

The women turn to me.

"For the girl," the large one says. She clicks her tongue again as she holds the shawl like a matador's cape, then wraps it around herself to model. When she spins, her earrings give off quick flashes of light.

"5000 pesetas," the toothless woman says. She extends her hand, demanding money.

When I shoo the women away, they return to Cecily and pull at the purse she wears diagonally across her chest.

"Leave me alone," Cecily says, then remembers her

Spanish. "*Déjame en paz.*"

"*Si, que nos dejen en paz,*" Ignacio says.

Cecily reaches into her bag. "Take this," she says, thrusting her hand at one woman, but Cecily lets go of the money before the woman can catch. The coins fall in the dust.

"*Puta rica,*" the heavy one says while her friend searches the ground.

"Let's get out of here," Ignacio says.

"*Puta madre.*" The woman grabs Cecily's wrist before she can get away. She slides her fingers under the bracelet, ready to snatch it off.

I pull the woman from Cecily and shove her to the ground. The coins in her apron pockets jangle as she falls. Her skirt flies up over her face.

"Shit. Where's the bracelet?" Cecily says, looking around her feet. "See if she's got it, Nick."

I hold the woman to the ground and pry her fingers open until I see her empty hand.

"Over here!" Ignacio yells on his knees. He passes the bracelet to Cecily. "Now go!" She clutches the bracelet and begins running up the hill.

When I get up, the standing woman reaches deep into her apron pocket and takes out a small pair of scissors. She holds the handle tight in her fist so that the blades point at me. I jump out of the way when she lunges in my direction. I don't feel it at first, but the scissors nick my arm, leaving a perfectly round bead of blood on my skin that starts trickling down to my elbow.

Ignacio yanks me up and we run to catch up with Cecily. Our feet crunch too loudly on the rocky ground, muffling all other noise, as if the background sound to a movie has been turned up to create a dramatic effect. A rock that the woman throws hits me in the back. I duck and block my head with my arms. Ignacio does the same. We keep our heads covered until we are out of reach. I look back down the road. The women have disappeared.

At first none of us speak when we arrive at the gates of the city. Ignacio bends over, his hands on his knees, trying to catch his breath. Cecily sits on the curb while I lick my handkerchief, then wipe the trickle of blood off my arm. Some of our fellow train travelers are gathering by the gates for tours. Beggars are spread out with their tales of woe written in Spanish and English on bed sheets or cardboard: I HAVE THE CANCER AND FIVE CHILDS and HELP ME, PLEAS, I LOST MY JOB AND NO HAVE HOME.

The guitarist who sat ahead of me on the way to Avila begins to play.

"You OK?" Ignacio asks.

"A tiny cut on my arm," I say. "But she really nailed the back of my leg with a rock. I wish I'd worn long pants."

Ignacio pours water on his bandanna and wipes at the redness on my calf.

"What about you?"

"Just shaken up."

Cecily studies the thin gold chain on her palm. "It broke at the clasp," she says.

"Don't worry," Ignacio says. "We'll fix it first thing when we get back to Boston."

"I wanted this afternoon to be perfect," Cecily says. "I had such high hopes."

"Everyone's safe," Ignacio says. "That's the important thing." He kneels in back of Cecily to massage her shoulders.

Cecily hasn't shut her eyes a full minute when the yodelers reappear, getting out of a taxi. The father is carrying a paper bag with a baguette sticking out. We watch the family take out their picnic: cheeses, cookies, tins of fish, oranges. The mother is on a blanket with the baby yodeler on her lap.

Cecily closes her eyes again, but opens them once more when the baby waddles over from his mother and stands in front of her. At first the baby just looks at Cecily, not even blinking. Then the yodeler starts to giggle, a perfect baby-boy giggle, the sort of giggle you might record for a doll that's supposed to laugh when you press his belly button.

Cecily puts her hands over her eyes. Her body heaves like she's gasping for air. Ignacio wraps his arm around her.

"What is the matter?" the father asks when he comes over to retrieve his son.

"*No se preocupe*," Ignacio says. The father carries the baby back to the picnic.

"He just put me over the top," Cecily says between breaths. "It's so fucking ridiculous. All he did was laugh."

"Here," Ignacio says. He hands Cecily his bandanna.

"It's insane," Cecily says, wiping her face. "The week was going so well, too. I was OK. The three of us were OK."

I touch her cheek. Her face looks gaunt, thinner than when we began our trip only five days ago.

"I'm sorry," I say.

Cecily doesn't respond. She closes her eyes and rubs the bracelet between the tips of her fingers, like a Spanish nun saying the rosary. Her bottom lip starts to quiver. She is whispering to herself, words as incomprehensible to me as the words she blurted in the delivery room while Ignacio and I urged her on through our green masks. And now, like then, she cries out suddenly: a piercing cry that makes the blood rush to her face. The yodelers look back at us again, the beggars stop their chanting for money, and even the stoned guitarist interrupts his music.

Ignacio cradles Cecily as her breathing slowly gets back to normal and the shaking stops. After a while she says she's stronger, ready to stand, so he helps her up and brushes the dirt off the back of her jeans. She falters when she starts to walk, as if she's been hit by a dizzy spell from rising too fast. Ignacio steadies her by the waist as they approach the gates.

"Wait," Cecily says. "I have to do something."

Cecily walks to a kneeling old beggar woman. She holds the broken bracelet at one end so it hangs like a hypnotist's watch. The gold glistens in the sun. The woman, her tired eyes opened wide, cups her leathery hands. Cecily releases the chain with a distant stare, as if following advice she hasn't quite taken to heart.

The woman laughs when she catches the chain. The smile Cecily returns is a flash of happiness: at least for that moment she knows how it feels to let go. She looks to Ignacio. "We can go inside, now," she says.

SUGAR BOY

Right before she died, my mother told me to wash the sugar off my arms and legs. It was mid-August, the summer between the fourth and fifth grades. By this time my mother had been in bed for about two weeks straight and only got up to go to the bathroom or have an occasional supper with me. All morning she'd been speaking so softly I had to strain to make sense of her, but when she talked about the sugar the words came out clear, as if she'd been storing air deep down in her lungs to help her say the most important things. "Sugar Boy," she said, "my little boy covered with sugar." Her long dark hair was gnarled against the pillow and as I stood naked by her side, I imagined that when my mother finally left her bed for good, those strands of hair might leave an imprint on the linen, like a fossil. "Sugar Boy, I need more water," she said. The bed was already surrounded by the glasses on the floor, some of them just about full. When I moved my arm some sugar fell off me and landed in a tumbler she used in the summer for her iced tea. The water made soft ping sounds that my mother couldn't hear.

Recently, I dreamed that all the water in my apartment was coming out blood red or the color of urine. At first, I didn't think about the water that surrounded my mother that morning, or about how my mother kept asking me to go down to the kitchen to fill up glass after glass, or even about how she called me "Sugar Boy" as I helped her wash down her pills. I thought about Roger as soon a I woke up. Sweet Roger, my ex-lover I hadn't spoken to for three weeks, whose voice I knew would soothe me. I called and told him about my dream. It was two o'clock in the morning and I was lying in bed in my boxer shorts.

"What are you doing calling me at this time of night?" Roger said. "You can do this sort of thing when you're seeing somebody, Denny, but we broke up. Remember?" Roger gave me one of his sighs of resignation that often followed his failed attempts at anger. "Look, if you really want my opinion I guess I'd have to say it all stems from anxiety over changing fluids with somebody. Are you seeing somebody?"

"No, that's not it. I know exactly what triggered it," I said. That afternoon I'd been arranging the window display in the bookstore when the janitor startled me by throwing a bucket of water against the glass. I imagined the water had splashed into my own space, on *me*, and I felt a churning in my stomach. I thought I might faint. "It's just so obvious," I said to Roger. "All I'm asking for is a little irony."

"Irony is out, Denny. We know this already, remember?" It was not the first time Roger had said this. At the

"Laughter in the Workplace" seminar where he and I met, we skipped the session on irony. Instead, we went to a mall in Framingham and watched the girls with sculptured hair walk by.

"Ironic, isn't it?" I'd said looking at the girls. "I mean, spending all that time to look so awful."

"Seeing something as ironic is no longer a sign of intelligence and wit," Roger said.

Elise, my boss at the bookstore, had insisted I go to the workshop. She'd recently promoted me to be one of half a dozen managers, but was concerned about my reserve and whether I could deal with my co-workers, so along with the promotion was the requirement for the seminar.

"It'll teach you to lighten up," she told me. Elise was a short-haired lesbian in her fifties who gave all her employees a joke-of-the-day calendar for Christmas and awarded a prize for the best April Fool's joke.

"But I have relationships," I said. "I don't need jokes. I can work with people. I'm not shy, either. I'm just a little short, so you just think of me as shy and powerless."

"We could all use a good laugh," Elise said. "And you don't have to be dour to go, you know. Look at me. I went last year. Where do you think I get all my ideas?" In the spring Elise did a window display with nothing but lesbian and children's literature called "Dykes and Tykes."

I went to the workshop, where I met Roger during a session called "The Good News Is, The Bad News Is: Firing With Wit." The participants were paired off to practice with each other. I had my eyes on a bearded man in his forties and was hoping I might have to fire him. ("The good news is I think you have the most amazing buns. The bad news is they won't be around here anymore.") In the end the work-shop leader put me with Roger, who flirted with me to keep his job in the improvisation and with whom I slept that night, and then, back in Boston, many nights after that. But Roger sensed my mind wasn't with him at all as we made love.

"Where are you?" Roger finally asked me our last night in bed together. He rolled on his side. Although in his thir-ties, Roger kept his body in shape from years of weight-training. He went to Dave's Gym to work the stair master and Nautilus after he taught his senior seminar. Roger was Head of the English Department at Bunker Hill. "Denny, I don't expect much from you, but can't you be present when we're in bed? Let's call it a day. I need more than your go-nads, nice as they are."

I left his apartment and didn't call him until the night of my dream. "Is that it?" Roger asked when I finished ana-lyzing. "So you call me at two in the morning just to tell me about your wet dream?"

"Well," I said. "I thought we might talk a little, too."

"Now you want to talk? I've been sleeping with Marcel Marceau and now he wants to shoot the breeze? Do me a favor and don't confuse me, OK? I'm in therapy to straighten my life out." I pictured Roger running his hands through his light brown hair, something he did when he let himself get mad.

I let go of the phone so it pressed between my ear and the pillow. I slipped my shorts to my ankles and kicked them to the floor, then reached to my night stand for a small bottle of liquid vitamin E. I poured a few drops in my hand and rubbed my body. When I reached my abdomen I felt the flabby folds and resolved to start doing sit-ups again. I lowered my hand.

"What am I hearing?" Roger asked.

"Nothing," I lied.

"Jesus. This is not a 900 number. This is Roger."

"It's just vitamin E. Don't worry. I'm coming down with a cold and my skin was feeling gross so I was just putting some on."

"Fine. Are we through for the evening?"

"I'm not sure but I think there's a slight possibility I might miss you a little."

"I'm tired of these games. I need a break. This whole thing has gone on too long, like Proust. If you want to call, call me in a few weeks, OK? We both need some time and some space."

I sneezed and pulled a tissue from the Kleenex box beside my bed.

"You really do have a cold," Roger said.

"I'll be OK."

"No, really, Denny. Take some Bufferin. Or Echinacea."

"I'm fine."

"And lots of liquids. I mean lots, like a glass of water every half hour or so. Whoops. Sorry about that. The water, I mean. I don't mean to stuff your dreams. Try juices. You'll be peeing the Amazon but it'll help, I promise."

"I know all this."

"I'm sorry. I don't mean to be your mother."

"Don't worry. I'll drink lots of water, Rog."

"You should sleep with a full pitcher beside you."

And that's when I finally I started to think of those glasses that surrounded my mother when she died. Now and then the picture had come back to me in a flash, and then it would disappear for months, maybe years, until I was fumbling in bed with some stranger, or even with Roger, groping and pulling my way to some pleasure. I couldn't always remember exactly how the glasses got there, or why my mother might have even wanted so much water. But I knew I was naked, and I knew the feel of wet sugar on my skin. *Just one more glass of water, Sugar Boy. Bring me one more.* Another glass to put next to the mug or the tall frosted glass that opened up wide at the top, the one my father used to fill up with Knickerbocker beer. He had left us the previous spring to live with the woman he'd met in his hat store, "The Mad Hatter," while she was buying a birthday present for her husband. A few months later my mother took ill, and her sister, my Aunt Josie, came every day to check on the two of us. "Your mother's a little blue," she told me. "She needs her rest." I really didn't know what being blue meant, and watched her face daily for subtle changes in color.

"Denny, are you still there?" Roger asked.

"I'm here." I ran an oily finger in a slow line from my pubic hair to my neck.

"Enough," Roger said. "You're hooking me in again. Do you really have a cold or did you just sneeze because you knew I'd worry and you wanted to keep me on the phone? Shit, I don't know what I'm saying anymore. Bye. Take care of your cold. That is, if you have one."

"Sure. Bye, Rog. Call me, OK?"

"**H**e's in therapy, huh?" Elise said the next day. "Well, that's the final death knell. No second chances for you, baby." She

was finishing her book display on vegetarianism and paci-
fism, she called *Let There Be Peas On Earth.*

"What do you mean?"

"What I mean is you can kiss any chance of getting
Roger back good-bye," Elise said. "I know from experience
that people always go into therapy to get out of relationships. Nobody ever says it, but that's the bottom line. Well,
if you ask me, I think it's time you found yourself a nice new
boy. You seemed happier when you were with that sweet
kid who worked at Towers. Rick, was it?"

"Ralph."

"Ralph, Rick, Roger, Raymond, Roberto. I can't keep
track of them," Elise said. "Come on up here and straighten
out the sign. Bring that book on gourds while you're at it."

I blew my nose hard before I picked up the book.

"If that cold gets too bad, you stay home tomorrow,
OK?" Elise said. "Now come on up here. You're still not
freaking out about the water splashing the window yesterday, are you?"

"No, I'm OK." I stepped onto the display with the gourd
book close to my chest.

"Because it's kind of fun here, really," Elise said. "Once
at a dyke march I actually bared a tit through the window.
The whole crowd cheered."

I edged myself away from the corner where I'd retreated
after the janitor had thrown the water. I remembered dropping my head between my knees and breathing deeply. Then
I looked up at Elise and tried to read her T-shirt, but the
letters across her chest appeared new to me, like the back-
wards and upside down *E*'s of an eye exam.

"I really thought you were going to lose it," Elise said

now. "Hand me that book on Gandhi, will you? I'll put it right next to the book on how spinach stops hair loss. Or do you think that's too obvious?"

"Sounds fine." I rose to my knees to give Elise a heavy volume with Gandhi's picture on the front, his bald head gleaming in the sun.

"So, you going to tell Aunt Elise why you went nuts yesterday? You almost drown as a kid or something?"

"I don't think so," I said. "We used to live in back of a pond in Lynn, but nobody ever went swimming there. It was more like a swamp."

"Well, maybe you were just having a bad day," Elise said.

"I guess."

I didn't tell Elise about how, for months after my mother died, I refused to run the tap or wash the dishes for my Aunt Josie, or how I didn't want to bathe and was sent home with a note from Mrs. Toomey, my fifth grade teacher, about my greasy hair. "You are *hydrophobic*," Aaron Kolinsky told me as if I were somehow contagious. Aaron Kolinsky was the son of an undertaker and sat next to me in school.

It rained for days after my mother died. I was afraid of that, too. It seemed that all the water I'd brought up to my mother was coming back down to me as a reminder of what I had helped her do. I was peeking through the doorway when I heard my mother speak in her groggy voice, then ring her small bell on the night stand.

"I need more water," she said. "I need a bucket for you to wipe my face. And I need another glass because I'm thirsty and have to take my medicine."

I ran downstairs. One glass. One bucket.

"Here," my mother said. "Put this on the floor." She handed me the glass she used to swallow her pills. "Wipe my forehead with a cloth and water." I dipped a face cloth in the bucket and wrung it out. I folded it across my mother's forehead. "Take a pill out of the envelope and put it on my tongue," she said. "It's OK. The doctor gave them to me so I could sleep." Her tongue had a white sheen to it, like she had just drunk milk. "Now the water. More water." I handed her the glass, but she couldn't hold tight so I tipped it towards her mouth to swallow the pill. Water dripped across her cheek and down to the pillow. "Put the glass down on the floor next to the others." She breathed deeply. "And the bucket, too. Fill the bucket again."

I had left the water running in the kitchen and the floor had started to flood by now. I took off my sneakers and socks and rolled up my pants as I splashed my feet on the floor. I ran up and down the stairs with more glasses.

"Denny," she finally said. "I'm getting cold now, like the heat is leaving my body through my head. Cover my head with something, will you?" I took off my shirt and wrapped it around her. "The water," my mother said. I poured some water across her lips. I saw that she had put another pill behind her teeth.

"Should I get more?" I asked, but when my mother moved her lips this time, nothing came out. I ran downstairs to the rising water anyway. This time I took off my jeans so the bottoms wouldn't get soaked. Suddenly I took off my undershorts, too, and sat in the water as if I were taking a bath. I got water all over myself, kicking and splashing like a baby. I rolled across the floor so I was wet all over, not just my legs and the smooth surface of my chest, but between my legs, too, and under my arms and in the folds of my ears. When I heard a groan from upstairs, I stood up and dripped for a while. I loved the sensation of something other than my clothes touching my skin. I walked to the cupboard where I found the bag of confectioner's sugar. I spread the sugar all over my body and across my face. I felt like I was dressing up in a costume, like I wasn't really me and wasn't really doing what my mother was asking me to do. I ran upstairs to her bedroom where she was still. I went to her side and touched her hand.

"You're white," my mother said.

"Sugar."

"Come next to me, Sugar Boy."

I climbed in bed and wrapped my arms around her, thinking she might move, but she didn't. I stayed with her a while longer, until I could no longer feel her breath. I rolled over and felt the little cotton knobs of the bedspread against my bare buttocks, then got off the bed and looked around me. The bed was surrounded by glasses now. Some were empty, some were half full, some were almost full. I held up a glass to the window as if looking for tadpoles in swamp water. *She must be dead because she doesn't need the water. She died right here, with this glass.* Even now I don't know why, only it seemed a good way to say good-bye to her, but I brought the glass to my lips and swallowed the water in one long gulp. I looked at my mother. I had left streaks of sugar across her face and hair. I blew the sugar off her forehead. It was like cleaning the dust off an old and broken doll from the attic.

Many years later, as Roger sat exhausted in his apartment before the first of three hospitalizations, I realized that what I had also left on my mother's bed was a moment close to intimacy, one I'd never know again. Intimacy had become solely maternal, or somehow connected with death; and when as a high school senior I learned that the French called orgasms "little deaths," I thought of my mother again in her bed and remembered what I said to Aunt Josie when I finally called her. "She took her pills. Now she isn't blue."

"**M**r. Peterson?" I said in a deep voice. "Mr. Roger Peterson? I'm calling to tell you that the book you ordered, *How To Get Him Back,* has finally come in."

"Denny, what do you want now?"

"What are you doing home from work? I thought I was going to get your answering machine."

"I'm depressed. I'm taking a personal day to stay home and watch Mary Tyler Moore." Roger had taped the entire MTM series from cable and arranged them by episode number in a bookcase.

"It's going into therapy," I said. "That never helps."

"How's your cold? I've been worried."

"It's in my chest now but I'll be OK."

"I'm sick, Denny."

That was all he had to say. We gay men really need to come up with a whole new language for degrees of illness because despite all the new drugs and cocktails and inhibitors, anyone who's sick these days is still dealing with death somehow, and you just can't use the same word for a cold or flu or even cancer. So all Roger could say was that he was sick—swollen glands, fever, diarrhea—and had been sick the night I'd called him about my dream.

"Fuck, Roger. Why didn't you say something?"

"I didn't find out until after we broke up," Roger said. "I had a few symptoms before, but nothing like this. I guess I didn't want to face it. We were so safe. You don't have to worry."

"I'm not worried about me."

"This all hit so quickly. I always thought it happened more gradually."

"And there you were harping on my cold."

"Projection, Denny," Roger said. "You should try therapy. You might learn something about yourself."

"I'm sorry, Rog. Jesus, I'm sorry. Fuck. That's all, just *fuck*."

"I just want to stay right here in my living room and watch Mary Tyler Moore throw her little beret up in the air. Really. If somebody told me I could live another thirty years or so but I'd have to spend it watching MTM reruns, I'd tell them it'd be OK. Isn't that pathetic?"

It didn't seem pathetic to me. I found the image touching, partly because I half believed Roger might have opted for that sort of life even if he wasn't given an ultimatum. He could be perfectly happy in his blue silk robe and stocking feet in front of the TV. I kept that picture of Roger with me as I began helping him with his first bout of illness.

Helping. That's what I told everybody I did for my mother the day she died. Word, of course, got out. The ambulance driver, Aunt Josie, and even the undertaker, Mr. Kolinsky, spread the story around.

"Dennis killed his mother He fed her all these pills," Aaron said one day at recess.

"I didn't," I said. "I just helped. I just did what she asked me to. I was only helping. I swear."

"And he had sugar all over him!"

"Well, your father's a sicko, Aaron! What's he doing earning money like that, taking a dead body and putting his hands where they shouldn't be?" I pictured Mr. Kolinsky with my mother's naked body on a table in front of him and had to close my eyes. "Why doesn't he just own a Shop Quick? Why does he have to be an undertaker, anyway?"

"Roger," I now said over the faint hiss of the phone. "What can I do?" The words sounded as though they came out easily, but the truth was that I waited a long time before I said them. I knew there would be things for me to do. Eventually there would be more trips to the bedside, more trying to tell the difference between sleep and death, more glasses of water, more *helping*.

"Just come and see me, Denny. OK?"

"*F*uck Mary Tyler Moore," Elise said when we got to Roger's apartment. I'd been visiting him almost every day for a week. Elise often came with me. Roger was watching the Chuckles the Clown episode. "Turn that thing off. I've got something better," She pulled out a porn movie called *The Son Also Rises*. "It's about a guy who leaves college to start a gay escort service with his father. The plot sounded interesting. Very literate, Mr. English Teacher."

"Better than Hemingway," Roger said. His voice was weak and dry. He kept a large plastic tumbler of root beer with a 7-Eleven logo on it next to the couch. When he sipped from the long straw, Roger let some soda spill across his lips to keep them wet.

Elise ejected MTM and put in a porn movie. Soon the three of us were watching a gang of men engaged in acrobatic sex. "Well, boys," Elise said after a while. "This cinematic experience is doing nothing for me. I'll go down to the store and get you some stuff you need, Rog. Root beer, right? Anything else you can think of?"

"Toilet paper," Roger said. "Get the really soft kind, if you can."

"Right. I'll be back."

When the movie got back to the plot, I turned to Roger. "I'll help you," I said. "Really. Not just now but later, too."

"Thanks, Denny," Roger said. "But you know, you could help me now. Go run and tell Elise to get some lozenges. My mouth tastes awful."

"I'll get something for you. Just hold on a sec."

I went to his kitchen and came back with a bag of sugar.

"Let me just spread this over your mouth, Rog. It'll taste real nice." I licked my fingers, dipped them into the bag, then touched his lips. "Open up," I said. I put more sugar on his tongue and wiped my finger along his gums. "There," I said. "How's that?"

"Nice, Denny. Sweet."

I pulled a small bottle out of my CVS bag.

"What's that?"

"Vitamin E." I poured some oil and slipped my hand under his robe. By now the boys in *The Son Also Rises* had taken their clothes off again. "You just keep looking straight ahead and I'll take care of the rest."

As I stroked Roger, I thought about how you can only get so close before something gets in the way. Latex. A TV screen. Oils. Skin. The past. The past: right after my mother died, I went to her closet and took one of her long chiffon nighties off the hanger. I pulled it over my naked, sugar-coated body and stood there, hoping the closeness would come back, but when nothing happened I ran through the house, up and down the stairs to the flooded kitchen, in and out of rooms, the chiffon of her gown brushing the inside of my legs. I was crying. That was the past, when, after I'd stroked and stroked a lover until he came, I might drop down and run my tongue along his stomach; but now, in the age of safety, I licked the sugar off his lips.

I was crying, now, too, and Roger, as surprised as I was, reached up and touched my neck to comfort me.

None of us knows anyone anymore, not even ourselves.

PAPER MAN

Jasper and I are sitting in a vinyl two-seater outside his office. He's is a big man and takes up most of the couch. I feel his elbow in my ribs. He's asked me to come here to talk to a Salvadorian refugee who's about to be thrown in jail. On the phone Jasper told me it was an emergency; he was handed this case out of the blue. He'd called everywhere and couldn't find anyone who spoke Spanish. I was his only hope.

What Jasper didn't say was that I was the obvious person to contact. He's been my friend since college and, a few years ago, was my lover for three months. He knows how hard I try to please and how I never say no. He knows I write thank you notes for everything, never pass up an opportunity to volunteer, and will hold an elevator door open even if I suspect someone might be approaching. In my early twenties, I was a social worker like Jasper, but I had to quit from lying awake with worry about the people I saw who were in such trouble. Now I teach Spanish but only on a substitute basis. My shrink tells me this will help me not get overwhelmed with my work.

"Will you speak to him for me, Guy?" Jasper asks now.

I sigh. I really don't like my name, which was also my father's. Who wouldn't resent being called Guy Jr. as a kid? When Jasper broke up with me, he sat me down and said he needed to love a more original guy. That's Jasper for you. He's written articles on the role of wit in psychotherapy. That's also me: I'm not a very original guy. For a while I tried asking people to pronounce my name in the French manner, so that it rhymed with *key*, like Guy du Maupassant, but nobody listened. So I'm still Guy in a world filled with fascinating, brand-named people. Who ever heard of a character named Guy? Guy Gatsby? Guy Copperfield? Guy the Obscure?

"I feel rusty," I tell Jasper now. "I'm nervous. There are so many words I don't know."

"You know plenty."

As always, I want to get everything right. I start listing all the words that I've either forgotten or never knew in the first place. "What about *kilt, raccoon, plaid, French horn*?" I say.

"Guy," Jasper says in his social worker voice, "those are not words you need to know."

In his office across from us sits Gustavo, who almost blew his brains out in the Fens last night. He had the misfortune of trying to pick up an undercover cop in the shrubs. Jasper says Gustavo needed the money, so he tried to hustle. Just when Gustavo was about to be arrested, he ran as fast as he could and ducked behind the rose bushes of a neighborhood garden. It was there that they found him pointing a gun at his head. Jasper wants me to explain to Gustavo that getting psychological help is the only way to avoid a mandatory year for handgun possession. Jasper wants to make the case that Gustavo's severely depressed.

"Let's go in," I say.

Gustavo's wearing jeans and a bright red T-shirt. He has some stubble on his face, but he looks more like one of those rugged GQ models than someone who's been up all night and didn't have the chance to shave.

"Hello," Jasper says.

On top of the table next to Gustavo are some sketches he's drawn of very muscular men with gleaming, smooth complexions and perfect teeth.

"Did you do these?" I ask him in Spanish.

Gustavo looks up for the first time since we've come into the room and nods to me.

"They're fabulous," I say. "I'm here to help. You can talk to me."

I reach into my coat pocket and take out a pack of cigarettes. When I offer one to Gustavo, he takes two, so I offer him a third.

About a year ago, I started doing some prompting at a community theater outside Boston. It seemed like a nice way to spend a few evenings, and I thought I might be able to meet some men. Last winter, I ended up dating a guy I'd fallen for while doing lines for *Pygmalion*. Things were going fine until my therapist, Dr. Ivanovna, pointed out that I'd actually fallen in love with Freddie Hill, the sweet, romantic young man he was playing, and not Garrett himself, who was cynical and didn't think twice about sleeping with other men while he was seeing me.

My sessions with Dr. Ivanovna haven't been progressing very well. I get the same questions over and over again I can't answer; Dr. Ivanovna gets more frustrated and begins to talk to me with the intensity of someone trying to empty a theater on fire. She is a Russian émigré who sometimes misses the finer points of English and is confused by our sayings that she mixes up freely. She once told me that Jasper and I were "two ships that go bump in the night."

"Why are you so afraid to love somebody real?" Dr. Ivanovna asks me today. We have been talking about Freddie Hill. "It is not good to love the make-believe person on the stage or the character in the book. They do not reciprocate the feelings."

I've already told her that as a kid I had a huge crush on both the Hardy Boys.

"What about Jasper?" I ask. "He was real."

"You gave so much to him that there was nothing left on the inside." She pounds her chest. "You disappeared. *Poof!* You gave with no return, like a bad investment, the same as when you fell in love with this Freddie the Hill and the Hardly Boys."

"Hardy," I say.

"You are like the chameleon," she says, pronouncing the *ch* like the beginning of *cherry*. "Whenever this Jasper was happy, you were happy. Whenever this Jasper was sad, you were sad. You do not feel for yourself. As they say, you must get the life."

"You mean get *a* life."

"You know what I mean," Dr. Ivanovna says.

*T*hese days I'm prompting for *The Comedy of Errors*. I get a little nervous about the Elizabethan language and whether I'll be able to read the lines with sufficient clarity. The nights I'm not at the theater I go over the pages we'll be rehearsing next, just so I'll know what everything means. Right now I'm reviewing the opening scene where Aegeon gives all the background information about the twins who were "so like the other as could not distinguish'd but by names." I've often wondered if twins not only look the same but feel the same way, too.

The phone rings. It's Jasper.

"I wanted to thank you for yesterday," he says.

"You're welcome."

Jasper hesitates before he speaks again, the way he does when he wants to ask for something. He's not really shy about asking, he just pretends to be: it's an acknowledgment that the favor is big.

"I was wondering if you could help me out a bit more," he says. In the past, helping Jasper out has meant any number of things: AIDS walks, making phone calls on behalf of some candidate he's working for, gathering signatures for Amnesty International to release some prisoner in Argentina. Once I drove with him all the way from Boston to New York City on the spur of the moment because he wanted to hear Allen Ginsberg at Columbia. Sometimes I think he was born at the wrong time; he should have come of age in the sixties, walked around naked at Woodstock, and protested the Vietnam War.

"Gustavo needs a place to stay for a few nights," Jasper says. "A shrink from the state came in and she's not buying the suicidal depression line. She says the whole gun-to-the-head routine was situational, nothing deep-rooted. For now, it's back to the courts. I was able to tap a few favors people owe me to post his bail."

I try to think what Dr. Ivanovna would want me to say. "Why can't he stay with you?" I ask.

"He could, but I don't know Spanish. Besides, he likes you. You got along so well with him. Please?"

Jasper always makes his requests sound so easy, as if he were asking you to buy Girl Scout cookies. He knows the way to my heart, so when I don't immediately agree, he tells me how Gustavo came to Boston to begin with, how he had fought the right wing in El Salvador, making it impossible for him to stay, how his father was killed and his mother and sister are living in hiding with a cousin who has a tiny house in a town outside San Salvador.

The sadness of Gustavo's life overwhelms me, but I know Dr. Ivanovna would remind me it's not my own sadness I'm feeling.

"So what do you say?" Jasper asks. "It's only for a few days, until I can convince the shrink to support him. You'd be doing good, Guy."

The way Jasper asks for favors, you'd rarely think they are just for him. They're for a bigger, common cause he fervently believes in. He makes you think you really can change the world.

"Mi casa es su casa," I say to Gustavo after Jasper drops

him off that night.

Gustavo looks around my apartment at the wall-to-wall shelves stuffed with books of all sorts: Spanish texts from my Master's program, biographies, and, mostly, the hundreds of novels I've devoured over the years. My desk is a mess with history papers from the class I'm substitute teaching for until the day after tomorrow, as well as some tutoring work I was preparing before Gustavo and Jasper came. There's a few books on Shakespeare and the prompter's copy of the play in a large red binder.

"Wow. So much paper," Gustavo says.

"I like to read."

"You are a paper man," Gustavo says, which sounds more poetic in Spanish: *hombre de papel.*

I picture the paper dolls we used to cut out as kids: white, generic things with no hands or feet or facial features.

"Can I get you a sandwich?" I ask.

Gustavo accepts. I toast some bread and take out the chicken salad I bought at Star Market the other day.

Gustavo eats in the chair where I usually sit. He's showered and shaved since I saw him in Jasper's office, and the rugged good looks of yesterday have given way to a softer beauty.

"Are you OK?" I ask. I worry that Jasper wasn't honest when he told me Gustavo wouldn't hurt himself. I watch him carefully as he cuts his sandwich in half. One slip across the wrists and it's over.

"I'm fine," Gustavo says. "I was just having a bad day."

"You mean you never planned to use the gun?"

"Never," Gustavo says. "I didn't know I could go to jail for having one. I wasn't really going to shoot. Not me, not anyone. People told me it could get dangerous down there, so I got a gun. I have this book that tells you where to find guys."

Gustavo takes out his wallet and shows me a page he's ripped out of the book. It's a section on cruising in Boston. The guide lists the usual places: The Boston Public Library, the boathouse by the Charles River, The Fens. At the end of each description are the letters AYOR, for "at your own risk."

"I bought the gun to protect myself," Gustavo says. "I really needed the money."

"We'll talk about money later. Right now you need to pull yourself together and take care of yourself."

"I need to meet with my lawyer tomorrow," Gustavo says. "What should I wear?"

Gustavo's slimmer than I am, though roughly my height. I go to the bedroom closet and take out three or four pairs of pants. I lay out some ties and hang a few sport coats on the bureau knobs. Gustavo selects the gray pants and the blue blazer to try on. The pants look big so I give him a belt that he wraps tightly around his waist. The jacket helps cover up the bagginess, too.

"Yes," I say. "This will work."

"Now I will look just like you," Gustavo says.

I put sheets and some pillows on the couch for Gustavo, and draw the shades so the sun won't wake him up too early in the morning. I worry that the couch isn't long enough for him, but Gustavo doesn't complain. I suppose he's slept in worse places, like train stations, park benches, the steps of an old church. I give him some Spanish books to read before he goes to bed. I show him where the light switch is.

"You are very kind to me," Gustavo says.

"I hope you sleep well," I say. "Anything else I can get for you?"

"No, thank you," Gustavo says. "I'm a little scared."

"Don't worry," I say, even though there's everything in the world to worry about.

I lie awake in my bed until I see the light go off in the living room. It's a cool April night and I've opened the window a crack. I hear the cars go by one at a time and count them, thinking it will help me fall asleep, but after a while I'm distracted by Gustavo tossing on the sofa. He mumbles words I don't understand. I can't fall asleep if I know he'll be awake all night; it's like trying to enjoy a movie with someone you know is having a miserable time.

"Gustavo?" I say at my bedroom door.

Gustavo sits up quickly and darts his head around, looking for someone to attach to my voice.

"It's just me," I say. "Why don't we switch?"

"I couldn't have you do that."

"It's only a few nights. Really, it's OK."

Gustavo doesn't resist. I show him to my room. It's been some time since he's had a bed, and he stretches his arms and legs out wide as if he were making snow angels.

I bring Gustavo to rehearsal one night. He sits next to me in the front row of the small theater that was once a church. The actors know their parts pretty well, but when the Second Merchant forgets one of the few lines he has, I give him the words forcefully, the way I think he should feel them, rather than without emotion as I have been asked to do.

"The hour steals on; I pray you, sir, dispatch!" I yell.

The director stops the run. "You're trying to act again," he says to me. He waves his hand towards the stage. "It's up to David to feel, for Christ's sake. We've gone over this a thousand times."

"I'm sorry," I say. "I'll do better next time. I just got carried away." I can't help it. I am liberated by words that are not my own.

"Maybe you need a break. Can your friend prompt?"

"He doesn't understand English."

"That doesn't matter," the director says. "That's what I want. Just words. The actors will take care of the meaning. Can he sound words out?"

I ask Gustavo; he nods. He's wearing a striped jersey I bought in Harvard Square a couple of weeks ago and looks better in it than I do.

"All they need are the first few words," the director says, "and only when they ask for a line."

I sit next to Gustavo as he follows the script with his finger. He only has to speak once, when the two guys playing Antipholis and Dromio of Syracuse drop their lines.

"I am trans—," Gustavo begins.

"I am transformed, master, am I not?" Dromio says.

"I think thou art in mind, and so am I," says Antipholis.

"Nay, master, both in mind and in my shape."

"Thou hast thine own form."

When the scene is finished, the director comes up to Gustavo and me. "Thank you," he says to Gustavo. "Guy, can you bring him along more often? That's how it should be done."

When we get back from rehearsal Gustavo takes out his sketch pad. We sit at opposite ends of the bed as he shows me drawings of some beautiful young men in various stages of undress. We tape his artwork on the walls of the bedroom, which seems less and less my own and more like Gustavo's. This morning we moved some Spanish books from the living room and put them next to the bed. Some of Gustavo's clothes are strewn on the floor. My alarm clock is now beside the couch.

Gustavo puts the sketch pad on his lap and looks at me.

"Your turn," he says.

I decline. I laugh at the thought of taking off my shirt. I'm ten years older than Gustavo and all his twenty-something men.

"Please," Gustavo says. "Just as you are."

Gustavo does not wait for me to answer but begins to draw me anyway. He works quickly. He asks me to turn my body and lift my chin.

I try not to stare back at him, but he's wearing gym shorts without a shirt. The pulse in my neck is pounding. When he finishes the sketch, he touches me right where the throbbing is.

"Are you OK?" he asks.

I don't answer right away. He bends to me and kisses my lips. I look at Gustavo's pictures on my walls and wonder whether these men were real men in Gustavo's life. I wonder what they were feeling when he drew them.

I want to prepare Gustavo a special meal before he leaves, which could be any day now. I never cook for myself, so I'm uncertain what to serve. I pick out things from the cookbook by the sound of their names, not by what's in them or what they might taste like. I'm a sucker for the letter z, so this night Gustavo and I have zucchini, ziti, Zabaglione.

"Some *zuppa*?" I say as we begin dinner. I say the Italian word for soup slowly, so that it floats around the candles.

As I ladle the soup, Jasper telephones.

"We need to talk," he says.

"I'm in the middle of dinner," I say. I've been planning to call Jasper, too. I've wanted to tell him about last night: how Gustavo kissed me, how we then made love, how sweet it was, nothing complicated. Gustavo needed someone to hold him; I held. If Jasper starts talking about boundaries, I'm prepared to tell him that Gustavo is not my client, that I haven't practiced social work in a decade. Besides, Jasper is not one to talk about living life between the lines.

Before I can ask Jasper if I can call him back, he says, "It doesn't look good for him. I don't know what else we can do."

"What do you mean?"

"No one believes he's depressed and that shrink who looked at him the other day isn't budging. It's going to court."

"Shit."

Gustavo looks up from his soup.

"I'm doing my best, Guy," Jasper says. "I'm trying to get him a good lawyer who'll take the case *pro bono*. If you can keep him a while longer, at least until they set a trial date, it'd be a real help."

I pause. To hell with Dr. Ivanovna, I think. I just won't tell her.

"Think big picture," Jasper says. "Think social justice."

"OK," I say. "Call me later."

"Who was that?" Gustavo asks when I sit back down to dinner.

"Jasper," I say.

"And?"

I look at Gustavo and can't lie. I tell him how things are with his case.

"They want to put me in jail," Gustavo says.

"You'll get a trial. It isn't completely hopeless."

"Yes it is. I don't trust the courts. They've never helped before."

"But that was in El Salvador."

"It doesn't matter. I've got to get out of here."

"And go where?"

"I can't stay in this country if I don't show up in court. They'll be looking for me."

"We're not talking about murder, Gustavo."

"It doesn't matter. Maybe they won't find me right away, but they'll find me eventually. I've got friends in Costa Rica. I could go there." At once Gustavo's eyes fill up. He looks younger than his twenty-three years. I begin to well up, too.

"How can I help?"

"I'll need a passport. I can't use my own. They'll arrest me at the airport."

I put my napkin on the table and go to the bedroom. I feel guilty going through the drawers without permission, so when I find my passport I leave quickly, stepping over a pair of jeans I used to wear.

"Here," I say to Gustavo who is still at the table, nervously tearing the crust off his bread.

"No," Gustavo says. "You've been so good to me. I don't want you to get in any trouble."

"I insist," I say. "Be me."

A few days later, Gustavo works on the passport with tweezers, a warm iron and a small sheet of plastic. He's done this for friends who needed to escape El Salvador, but it's still tricky. I watch him lift my own photo to replace it with one of his we had taken earlier in the day. He works under a small bright light in the kitchen, like a scientist examining slides. He uses the tiniest bit of glue so as not to ruin the picture.

"Here," Gustavo says, handing me the passport. I open to the photo of Gustavo with my name beside it. He's done a good job. I have to hold the passport up to the light to see even the slightest evidence of tampering.

We rehearse the airport scene that night, using the new passport he's made. I play the ticket agent and Gustavo plays me. We do this in English. I teach Gustavo to say as little as possible, and for the most part he is able to say the words with not much of an accent. I rattle off a series of questions about his citizenship, luggage, things he might declare. Finally I put a piece of paper in front of him, just in case they should require a signature.

"Please sign here," I say.

Gustavo writes quickly, providing the name he has practiced over and over. He ends with a dramatic wave of his hand.

Two days later and we're on our way to the airport. The morning is bright and sunny. I imagine Gustavo arriving in

San José in weather that isn't much different from what's here in Boston. I drive as carefully as I can since I don't have my license anymore. Last night Gustavo put his photo on it, the same way he doctored the passport, in case they ask for a second I.D. at the gate.

"I'll be OK," Gustavo says to me as we pull into Central Parking. I take his bags out of the car and flip his duffel bag over my shoulder.

"Have you got everything?" I ask in English so Gustavo can practice before we get to the terminal. "Ticket? Passport? License? Let me see everything, just to be sure."

"Don't worry," Gustavo says, also in English. "I'll be fine."

"Take this," I say. I hand him an envelope with $100 inside, then do a final check to make sure my name is on the luggage tags.

"Please say good-bye to Jasper for me," Gustavo says, "And thank him."

I don't know what I'll say to Jasper yet, whether I'll admit to helping Gustavo leave or tell him he slipped out during the night. I worry about the bail money Jasper will lose, but if anyone should understand that Gustavo had to leave, it's Jasper.

I watch Gustavo put his bags beside the counter and take out his ticket. The ticket agent asks Gustavo a few questions. I see Gustavo shake his head no, then take out his wallet and show her my license. She looks at Gustavo, then looks at the photo, then looks at Gustavo again. When I see her smile, my breathing returns to normal, as if I'd finally stepped out of an elevator that has dropped much too quickly. We've done it. Gustavo waves me towards him and we walk together to the metal detector.

Gustavo reaches into his bag. "Here," he says in Spanish again. "For you."

It's the drawing of me he did. I'm surprised at how formal the sketch looks: just me from the neck up, like a high school yearbook photo. I lack the spontaneity of the other men he's drawn.

"Good-bye," I say. "How will I know you're OK?"

"I'll be in touch," he says. He holds up his passport. "If something happens to me, you can always check the newspaper for your obituary."

"Very funny," I say.

Gustavo kisses me on the cheek. For a moment I consider holding tight to his wrist and asking him to stay. "We'll figure things out so you don't have to leave," I want to say, but he's already through the gate. A sadness starts to settle in but I catch myself and think about all I have to do today: report a lost license, apply for a new passport, prompt a dress rehearsal this evening.

I walk past the ticket agent and head for the garage. The airport seems empty, as if everyone else in the world is already where they should be. As I stop at the glass doors, I realize that in my nervousness I've crumpled Gustavo's drawing. I open up the paper. The lines are now smudged and so many wrinkles cross my face I doubt you'd even know it's me.

THE LAST WARM DAY

The summer my father opened up a convenience store in the bottom floor of our house, I saw someone dead for the first time, a man who had drowned off the shore of Flax Pond. It was really only the foot I saw, in an ankle-high sneaker caked with mud, as the firemen dragged the body up through the crowd to the ambulance parked in the sand. I was twelve then, skinny, with dirty blond hair that stuck to the sides of my head from the Red Sox cap I wore all day. Ned, my father's best friend, had brought us to the pond for a motor boat ride. We'd spent the last week unpacking cartons of cat food, spaghetti, Band-aids, canned potatoes with green and white checked labels, and enormous boxes of Kotex. The boat ride was supposed to give us a break from the store. We could have walked to the pond, but Ned had a convertible. The breeze cooled us off as we drove through Wyoma Square to his house and dock by the water.

We pulled up and saw the firemen dragging the bottom of the pond in their rowboats. People were lined up along the shore. The word had gotten out that they were looking for a man named Jack Manetti. A woman a few years younger than my mother sat on a rock near the water, crying. Two men stood behind her. They must have brought her straight from work because she was in a waitress uniform, the kind they wore at the Clam Plate, the seafood restaurant right across the Peabody line. The woman dropped her head into her hands and kept it there while her body heaved. She twisted the heels of her white work shoes into the sand but she couldn't stop shaking.

Nobody dared look too long at the woman except my mother. She was tall enough to see over the crowd if she stood up a little on her toes. She looked beautiful above everyone, the sun picking up the deep red highlights in her dark hair. She kept her eyes fixed on the rock until the woman lifted her head from her apron for a breath. That's when the woman caught my mother's stare. My mother pressed her lips tight and shook her head slowly, as if to let the woman know how sad she was for her. Then my mother turned to the water. A scuba diver surfaced and flipped his mask up to talk to somebody in a boat. Soon all the boats stopped, almost simultaneously.

"They got him," Ned said. "They use walkie-talkies to let each other know."

My father looked at me. He was blind in one eye and that blind eye was bright and clear. It wasn't lined up straight with the other eye. It seemed to have lost its muscle, and had, over the years, moved its focus off to the side. I believed it could pick up things the rest of us couldn't see.

"Sam, I'm going to get you out of here," my father said.

"You see a dead man once and that's something you'll never forget the rest of your life." He reached for me, but he was a small man with pale, weak hands that couldn't hold tight. I wriggled away.

"Wait a minute," my mother said. "You can't keep something like that from him forever. He's going to have to see it sometime."

I knew it wasn't me my mother was thinking about. She was the one who wanted to see the dead body. The crowd gathered around the boat as it pulled up to shore. Just then the woman on the rock screamed so hard I thought the sound might ripple the water clear to the other side. My mother pushed her way to the front and looked down. That's when I saw the man's sneaker dragging through the sand. It wasn't enough to shake me up like my father said it would. I wasn't even convinced the man was actually dead right then. For a long time afterwards I wondered how the woman on the rock knew it was time for her to cry.

*T*his was 1968. Only a few months earlier someone had shot Bobby Kennedy in California. I think I believed it when they said he was dead. I saw his face close up. The newspapers had pictures of him on the floor, a pool of blood around his head. My father was taking me to school when we heard the news on the radio. At first my father thought they were talking about his brother. "They ought to let us forget about that for a while," he was saying. Then the man on the radio mentioned Bobby's name. My father slammed his fist against the wheel and said, "What the hell is happening?" He pulled a U-turn right in the middle of the road and sped back home where we watched *The Today Show* all morning long. A doctor had a model of a skull on his desk and pointed to where the bullet entered. When they announced Kennedy had died, my father's eyes filled up and he left the living room.

My father wasn't a man who took to evil in the world easily. He just wasn't that strong. My mother was the one who got the newspapers delivered to our house. My father said he didn't want to read about all the bad things that were happening every night when he got home from work. He didn't even like to go out that much. The way he talked you'd have thought that every time a person ventured more than a few miles away from home something terrible happened.

After the assassination, my father began dreading his morning drive down Route 128 so much that at the breakfast table he'd hold tight to the handle of his coffee cup even when he wasn't lifting it to drink. His arm would tremble and the cup clinked against the saucer. Out of those anxious mornings came his idea of turning part of our house into a small store. In the course of a few short weeks he'd bought out the lease of the tenants below us, had the walls knocked down, built shelves, applied for his sales permit and ordered enormous freezers from a company in Michigan, all so he wouldn't have to leave home for the Polaroid plant in the morning.

At the store, while my mother and I were stacking boxes and cans for the opening, my father took care of the paperwork. I liked seeing my father in control. We had to treat the store like a business, he said, even though it was a family-run place. This meant that he wrote out schedules for my mother and me and typed a list of "employee guidelines" for us to follow. We couldn't chew gum, were expected to wear clothing that was "neat, clean, and in good repair," and had to knock before entering his office out back. The office was small with an overhead light and a door that rested horizontally across two piles of cinder blocks for a desk. Inside the room it was damp, and my mother hardly ever went in there on account of her asthma. My father had to weigh the important papers down with cans of creamed corn so the corners wouldn't curl up from all the humidity.

We opened in August. With the stacking done, my work slowed down and I got thinking about the drowned man now and then. The day after he drowned, they printed his high school graduation picture on the front page of the *Lynn Item*. In this picture he was smiling in a jacket and tie. The way the light hit, he looked like he had perfect skin. My mother's voice shook when she said he lived right next to the beauty parlor a friend of hers ran. His older brother went to St. Mary's High with Ned. Hearing these things didn't make the man any more real to me. Bobby Kennedy was killed a good three thousand miles away but at least I saw him on TV after he fell. I had to picture the drowned man before I understood why my mother was upset. I didn't know if I was doing a good job imagining him or not. I plastered the man's hair back with water. I took off the jacket he was wearing in his class picture and opened up his shirt collar. I put some mud on his arms and scratched up his face to make him real.

My new job at the store was to watch out for shoplifters. My father showed me how to rearrange loaves of bread so I could secretly monitor people I thought might steal, but the only person I ever saw taking anything without paying was my mother. I don't know if you'd call that stealing.

She'd sneak a bottle of suntan lotion into her beach bag along with some Virginia Slims right before Ned came in on his lunch break to ask if anyone wanted to go on a boat ride. He wore sunglasses and a light blue cotton hat with a brim that went all around his head. His flip-flops clicked against his heels when he walked.

"Flax Pond Cruises leaving in ten minutes," he said. He took off his hat and made a formal bow, one arm across his chest.

"You wouldn't mind, would you, Al? Even an old slave driver like you has to let me go every now and then," my mother said. She ran upstairs and changed her clothes. Because the rules said she had to look nice at the register, she'd taken out some old dresses she hadn't worn in the longest time and brought them to the cleaners. That particular day she'd been wearing a cream-colored dress that clung to her legs. Around her neck was a scarf with tiny flowers.

"Al, you come along if you want," Ned said. He turned to me. "Your father's afraid of water. You know that, don't you, Sam? We just ask him to be nice." Ned let out a laugh. He showed his large white teeth when he opened his mouth. A thick lock of hair fell across his forehead. Ned was tall with a peak to his hair. He had high cheekbones and a hawk nose that made him look a little threatening when you first saw him. He pushed his hair in place and plopped the hat back on his head.

That day it was hot even in the convertible. I put a towel across the back seat so the vinyl wouldn't burn my legs. My mother's hair blew across her eyes as Ned drove. She gathered her hair and wrapped it around the back of her neck so it fell over her shoulder.

At the pond, my mother slipped off her Bermuda shorts and blouse. Underneath she had on her new black bathing suit. She took out her suntan lotion and squirted some on her hand. She rubbed the lotion in little circles right above her breasts. She rubbed some on her face, but never touched her lips, which were thick and curved, softened by the pink lipstick she wore.

"Let's shove off, Sam," Ned said.

"Just a sec," my mother said. She settled herself in her seat, then went through her bag taking out one thing after another as if doing an inventory for a long trip.

I sat near the edge of the boat and pushed against the dock with my foot. Splinters fell into the water. Ned opened up the motor until we reached the other side of the pond. He slowed the boat down and brought us to an isolated cove. We drifted a while. Ned put on the transistor radio. Glen Campbell was singing "Gentle on My Mind" but static got in the way.

"And one of my favorite songs, too," my mother said. "Isn't that always the way?"

Ned shut off the radio. All I could hear were the little splashes of water against the boat. I got thinking about the drowned man again. I wondered if we were anywhere near where he went under.

"Did you see the guy who drowned up close?" I asked. "Did you really see him dead? His face, I mean?"

"Forget about him," Ned said.

"Of course I saw him," my mother said. She shook her head and let her hair fall down her back.

"I was just wondering what he looked like because I didn't see him."

"You haven't seen anybody taking things from the store, either, but it happens all the time. Ten or fifteen dollars a week, you know. You haven't caught a soul yet."

She was right. I played with loaves of bread and restacked canned goods every time somebody was in an aisle more than a minute or two, but I never caught anybody. I walked up and down trying to imagine what certain people might steal but, as far as I knew, nobody took anything that wasn't paid for unless you counted my mother's cigarettes and lotion.

I put my hand in the water and swished it around. The water was cold. Ned took off his T-shirt. Little swirls of hair on his chest stuck together with sweat. He flipped his sunglasses up over his head. He was about to lace his fingers behind his neck when he saw me with my hand in the water, looking down.

"You're still thinking about that guy, aren't you, Sam? Well, the guy was drunk. He had a six pack before he went into the water. He was asking for trouble. Nothing can happen to you out here. Just have a good time."

Then, without warning my mother or me, Ned slipped off his slacks and underpants and stood at the side of the boat, naked, facing the water. I tried not to look, but couldn't help keep my eyes fixed on his body since I'd never seen a naked man before, not this close anyway, not even my father.

Ned jumped feet first into the water. My mother screamed, then laughed. I pulled my hand out of the water. We waited for Ned to come up. All I saw were the ripples he made when he jumped in. The boat rocked back and forth from his splash. When he finally surfaced on the other side, he folded his arms across the side of the boat and put his chin on his hands. His shoulders were deep brown. The rest of his body was blurred underwater, but I could still make out the white of his backside glowing beneath the surface. My mother stretched her legs in front of Ned. She tapped her feet in the puddles and splashed some water in his eyes. Ned cupped a little pond water in his hands. Then he reached over the boat and let the water drip on my mother. Ned gently blew drops of water down her leg. The water rolled easily over the suntan oil.

"You see that, Sam?" Ned said. "We're as safe as you can be here. Nobody'll drown around here."

"I guess you're right," I said. I wasn't sure it was safety I was looking for, but I didn't say that to Ned. I wanted to know how you could tell when a man was dead, when you give up blowing air into his lungs to get him breathing again. I knew some people went through life knowing things just by the way they felt. I read that some people could spot a shoplifter by the way he breathed or whether his cheeks went red while he was holding something in the aisle. That was all the evidence they needed. The crowd around the pond didn't have to see Jack Manetti up close to believe he was dead. They didn't even blast the siren when the ambulance pulled away because nobody was in any hurry to get a dead man to the hospital. They tooted a few times to move people out of the way, then pulled out of the sand and drove along the street like everyone else.

*F*or a while Ned came by all the time to take my mother and me for rides during our lunch breaks. We missed a few days in September when he had to go to a convention for dental lab technicians in Chicago. He brought me back a large pair of false teeth that clattered when you wound up the little white handle on the side. My mother got a funny looking necklace made of long white plastic teeth, each strung individually. Each tooth had a letter on it, so when you turned all the teeth to face out they spelled "Evelyn."

Things changed during Ned's trip to Chicago, though. We didn't do as good a business over Labor Day as my father had hoped, and so one day he brought in an accountant for advice. The accountant was still in the back room when I got home from school one day. He had a cigar in his mouth and was punching out some numbers from the account sheets my father prepared. I didn't like the feeling he might find something out about us even before we knew it ourselves. On his way out the accountant said, "Well, it's bad all right. Sure, I've seen worse but you guys are still losing your shirts."

My father spent the next morning coming up with a five-point plan to boost our profits. He called my mother and me into the back room.

"My asthma, Al," my mother said. "It's not good for me in there."

"It'll only take a minute," my father said. He hung a "closed" sign on the door and he followed us down the center aisle. Once we were inside, he shut the door. "Turn around. I want both of you to read this. You've got to know these rules by heart." My father folded his arms across his chest and looked towards the door where he had taped his five points. He'd printed them neatly in red magic marker on white poster board:

1. We will have a weekly sale of one big item to bring people into the store. They will buy more things. We will make more money.

2. We will buy a large circular mirror to hang over the door. This will give Sam a better chance of catching the shoplifters he's been missing. Sam should now be able to catch two (2) shoplifters every ten (10) business days. This is not an unreasonable expectation for a twelve (12) year old.

3. As the cold weather comes this fall, heating will be used *efficiently.* Sweaters and thermal underwear will be made available to both employees.

4. We will remain open until 11:00 instead of 9:00 for a period of four (4) weeks on a trial basis and compare revenues during that time and the month of August.

5. Employees will no longer be permitted to leave the premises during lunch. Further, lunch will be restricted to thirty (30) minutes. No visitors will be allowed during this time.

On his knees that night, the thick red marker in his hand, my father printed signs to let people know what sales were coming up: pantyhose one week, then orange juice, frozen pizza, tonic. He gave me a little blue pamphlet he'd gotten from the accountant about shoplifting. The pamphlet was ten pages long and on each page was a drawing of the type of people I was supposed to suspect. They were people with baby carriages or little two-wheeled shopping carts they dragged behind, people in big coats, couples who split up and went down two different aisles. I learned the list. I didn't want this to be like the drowned man. I didn't want people telling me something was happening that I couldn't see for myself.

Ned found out about the end to the boat rides when my father took him out back to show him the list of rules. I heard Ned chuckle so as not to seem disappointed. He came out smiling but it wasn't the type of smile I was used to seeing on him. His lips were pressed together and he was nodding in that polite way people do when listening to strangers they're obligated to hear.

I was surprised that at first my mother seemed happy with these new rules. She filled her life with little things to do in the store. She checked the candy bars three or four times a day to make sure the labels were facing out, wiped the tops of the canned goods with a wet cloth, scoured the newspapers to see if anyone was offering a better sale on 7-Up than we were. The new details of her life took the edge off her; she was no longer the woman who needed to break through the crowd to see Jack Manetti dragged out of the water. She worked right through lunch time, when Ned used to take us to the pond, and she ate when I got home from school later in the afternoon.

We still saw Ned, but only now and then. He stopped by to watch the Red Sox on TV with my father. At first my mother tried to treat Ned like a normal customer but eventually she gave in to his charm. She sat on the stool behind the counter and smiled at him. She stretched her legs out and threw her shoulders back like she did in the boat the day Ned went swimming and I saw him without anything on. Sometimes I had a hard time getting that picture of him out of my mind, and, as uncomfortable as it was for me, I'd have to make sure I looked Ned in the eyes when he visited the store. But soon the joking would start between Ned and my mother. Ned asked for a pack of Larks then claimed he said Pall Malls. He accused my mother of short-changing him. And sometimes my mother would. She told Ned he'd only given her a one and not a five. She dropped her hand below the counter where Ned couldn't see and rolled the five dollar bill up like a cigarette. She slid it in her shoe. She dared him to come look for the money.

Ned pulled his pockets out so they hung empty to his sides. "Nothing," he said. "What's a man to do?"

When Ned left to go upstairs to watch the game with my father, my mother sat, still and quiet. It took a customer putting change down on the counter to get her to move. I watched her for a while, then put my mind back on the store. I took to memorizing where everything was stacked. To get to sleep sometimes I'd start in the row farthest away from the cash register and list one thing after another. My father could name anything in the store and I could tell him what was on either side of it, right above, and then under-neath.

Sometimes my mother started to wheeze—slowly at first, her hands sliding over the counter top to steady her-self from the long, loud breaths that made her whole body quiver, as if the little air she was taking in was all her body could hold. I searched the store for her asthma inhaler and then, if I couldn't find it, gave her the next best thing. I brewed some coffee for her at the small breakfast counter where in the morning people poured their own paper cups to go. The doctor said the caffeine kept her adrenaline going. My mother sipped carefully and her shoulders dropped, the tension gone. When she spoke it was in a whisper, and I lowered my voice to hers so that even when we were talking again we could still hear Ned cheering at the game on TV upstairs. He yelled when the ball was dropped or a pitch swung on and missed, and he stamped his feet with his deep laugh when the game would go his way.

In October some geese landed in our back yard, stayed for five days, and then left. They woke me up in the morning before my mother had a chance to come to my room. It was Indian summer. There had been a frost in late September and now, suddenly, a July heat came that seemed even hotter because it was out of nowhere. On Saturday, Ned stopped by at lunch for the first time since my father told him the new rules. The geese honked as the convertible pulled into the driveway. He left the car running when he got out. He leapt to the top of the porch without using the stairs.

"Flax Pond Cruises!" he yelled before he even got inside.

My father came out of the back room. He had a pencil behind his ear and was rubbing his hands together, as if to massage his fingers after writing for a long time.

"The Sox aren't on, Ned," my father said. "The season's over."

"You got to let them go for one more ride in the boat," Ned said. "It's the last warm day of the year. You wait now and we won't have a day like this till next June." Ned took the towel he'd draped around his neck and held it out like a matador's cape. He waved it so as to entice us.

My mother was at the counter. She had a coffee cake in front of her she'd taken off the rack across from the register. She opened the package with her teeth, then played with the cellophane so that it crackled while we waited for my father to say something.

"Her asthma, Ned," my father said. "There's a little air conditioner in here to make the place nice and cool. Air needs to be light for her, you know. It's what the doctor says."

My mother stopped touching the cellophane. She took a clipboard out from under the register with the names of all the brands of cigarettes listed. She turned around and started counting the cartons of each brand that were piled behind the counter. "Some other time," my father said.

"You old killjoy, you," Ned said. He laughed, but his body had grown stiff. He stepped on one end of the towel and pulled tight on the other end. Then he lifted his foot, yanked the towel up with a snap, and flipped it over his head so it hung over his shoulders again. He turned and left. When he opened the door, I could feel the heat coming in. The geese honked some more when Ned got in the car and drove off.

Later that night, while my father was upstairs, my mother went to find Ned. I know this even though she didn't tell me. She put a "closed" sign on the door and asked me to wait quietly inside. I watched her walk down the street. She stopped a few houses down from us and took her compact out of her bag. She touched her hair on the sides and dabbed some lipstick on her top lip. With her finger she spread the lipstick evenly around her mouth. I saw her walk off.

All my mother told me about where she had gone was that she needed some air. She'd been feeling a little dizzy, and she needed to get outside. "That air conditioner," she said, "makes the air stale. It just got to me." On her legs and arms were red puffy marks of mosquito bites. She scratched them once or twice, but they didn't seem to be bothering her much. Her breathing had gotten worse while she was away, and, sitting on the stool, she twisted the bottom of her blouse to keep her arms steady. She leaned over and clutched her knees. I got some calamine lotion from the shelf near the wall and rubbed some on her arms. I told her to go through her bag for some medicine. She reached inside without looking and took out a lighter and her compact, but no spray. I made coffee. My mother's hand shook when she held the cup, and some coffee spilled on her skirt. She looked down but didn't wipe it off.

"I was thinking about Jack Manetti," she said. She paused and took a deep breath. "His wife, really. That woman on the rock." When she spoke next all her breath seemed to come back to her, at least for a moment. "It's a terrible thing to lose somebody like that. A terrible, terrible thing. Don't you think so, Sam?"

"Your coffee," I said. I remember taking her arm and bringing the cup to her lips. The cup had pink marks from her lipstick on the side. "Just drink."

By morning it had gotten cooler outside, cool enough for sweaters. The geese left quietly at sunrise. The yard was empty, save for some feathers and a few apples, half-eaten and brown. The grass had been torn up. I knew the geese had gone before I ever looked out the window. The idea just came to me in bed. *You don't need proof anymore.* I knew that thinking this way was a turn for me, and that once I started to guess my way through life it would be hard to go back to needing evidence all the time. It really started the night before, with my mother and her mosquito bites and coffee. After that I didn't need proof to know that Jack Manetti had died, or Bobby Kennedy; that people had been stealing things from the store right under my nose all summer; that my mother lost the man she loved more than anyone else in the world, and from then on she, too, would have to guess her way through life—Ned's life—wondering where he'd gone and what he was doing. He did stop by once or twice early that winter, but that was it. He left town shortly after Christmas, and all I knew was that it was the last I'd see of him for a very long time.

Just Looking

Veronica and I used to play a game to come up with depressing titles for her memoirs if she ever decided to write them—names like *It Could Have Been Worse* or *If There's a Song in My Heart, Then Kurt Weill Must Be Singing*. If I produced the saddest name, I'd get the dedication as well as the chance to ghost write her life. "It'd be the perfect job for you. Peter," she said to me. "You're really an *as told to* kind of guy."

I didn't point out to Veronica that this was a job I already had in her life. Lately she'd been calling me two or three times a day to ask my advice. She'd just lost her third job in two months and had a few days earlier discovered that the lover she called the Man of Her Dreams was stripping his clothes off down to a little gold pouch at a gay night club, then cruising the place after his show.

I was the one who gave her the news, since it was Theo and I who had caught his act at *Atlantis* the weekend before.

Now Veronica was not only jobless, but most likely love-less, too. Even her therapist, whom she had been seeing for at least ten years, couldn't help her.

"He told me to scream at chairs. Empty ones, where all the men in my life used to be," Veronica said. She and Stephen and I were making our way through a photography exhibit at the Institute of Contemporary Art, a museum that was a series of small rooms with narrow entrances. I might not have noticed this if I weren't pushing Stephen in his wheelchair. He'd had a stroke late last spring, a week after his forty-ninth birthday. Today was Saturday afternoon, one of the few times in the week Stephen was allowed out of the rehab hospital.

"So have you tried it?" Stephen asked Veronica.

"Tried what?" Veronica asked.

"Screaming at chairs," he said.

"Once or twice. But I decided I'd do better with a bag of Cheese Curls and some Valium," Veronica said. "It worked last night, anyway."

"Then if it worked so well, maybe we don't have to go through with this afternoon," I said. I was hoping she might come to her senses and give up her plan for me to meet Chad to "straighten things out," as she put it. I was positive the stripper was the same guy Veronica brought to meet Theo and me at lunch a few weeks back. There was no need for me go with her today to confirm what I already knew.

Veronica called Chad anyway and suggested they meet at the old zoo near her apartment building. Her father had taken her there all the time when she was a child, and now, as an adult, it had become her favorite place to talk. That the zoo had run out of funding and was closing down was just another great disappointment in Veronica's life these days. I'd come out to her there five years ago, in a perfectly staged moment right by the flamingos. Veronica kissed me on the cheek, said how happy she was for me, then burst into tears, whimpering something about how I'd always been the Man of Her Dreams.

"I need you, Peter," Veronica said now. "If you have any kind of a heart in that chest cavity of yours you'll come with me this afternoon." She pulled her long red hair over her shoulder, then stopped in front of a photo. "Hey, you guys, look at this one."

All the photos in the room were of the same young man named Lyle in various stages of undress. We were now looking at a photo of Lyle wearing nothing but an unbuttoned bowling shirt and holding a hoola-hoop. The photo was called *Retro Lyle*. He had the smooth, defined body of a Greek Olympian and the lighting in the photo made his skin glisten like water.

"This sure beats my book group," Veronica said.

"What were you supposed to read?" Stephen asked. His life in the hospital had been reduced to videos and books.

"Oh, we never read anything," Veronica said, staring at Lyle. "We dropped the book part a long time ago. Now we just sit around and drink wine and talk about sex. We keep calling it a book group to sound legitimate, I guess. They'd kill me if they ever knew I was skipping out to meet a man. Besides, I might have to rush in for a second interview this afternoon at that boutique in Cambridge. They said they'd call today. I have to check my messages later on."

Another photo of Lyle caught Stephen's eye. "Oh, my," he said. He repositioned his wheelchair. "I haven't seen a naked man for six months." He tended to talk less since the stroke, and more slowly, too. He was still in speech therapy to work on his public speaking. Sometimes when I'd visit, he'd read to me, just for practice. He wanted to feel confident when he returned to the Unitarian Church where he was minister. He hoped to be back in the pulpit by Christmas.

Stephen and I grew up together in Beverly. He was four years older than me, and as a kid I had a crush on him. When he took me for a ride in his car the day he got his license, it felt more like a date than anything I think I've ever experienced. These days it was hard for me to be clear about my feelings for Stephen. I loved Theo, but he was ten years younger than I was. It didn't bother me that he ate Lucky Charms for breakfast, but I did want to talk about more than Brad Pitt's movies or the latest dance track at Chaps. After Stephen would practice reading to me in the hospital, we'd talk for a while. We had read the same books, liked the same operas, known the same people when we were kids. Theo barely remembered Woodstock.

"Why don't I ever meet guys like that in the personals?" Veronica asked as she looked at the photo with Stephen. "Lyle would never be a *Carte Blanche* man." *Carte Blanche* was the name of the dating service Veronica had used before she met Chad. "A few weeks ago I met this guy who introduced himself as a pet therapist. I wasted all that time and money to meet Lassie's shrink."

Sometimes I thought Veronica put down her $500 for a *Carte Blanche* man so she could keep telling us amusing stories about the fools she was meeting. That way, she could feel funny and superior at the same time.

"Aren't you too young to remember Timmy and Lassie?"

Stephen asked.

"Reruns," Veronica said.

"I bet Timmy was gay," Stephen said.

Veronica sighed. "There's one more guy I can't go out with."

"Why do you even need a dating service?" I asked. "You're smart, witty and beautiful. What more could a guy want?"

"You are a friend, Peter," Veronica said. "Maybe the two of us will be lovers in another life."

"You'll find a man," I said. "I did."

"Which now makes you the only married man I know who I haven't dated," Veronica said as she sat on the floor.

Stephen wheeled his chair to get a closer look at *Lyle with Volvo*. "So what do you guys think?"

"Doesn't do much for me," I said. I tried not to sound self-righteous, but I was tired of young, smooth hunks gracing the pages of every gay magazine I picked up. Where were the guys like Stephen and me? It didn't help that I recently found Theo's stash of porn hidden in his bottom drawer when I was putting away the laundry. I was surprised at how hurt I'd felt. Theo assured me he still found me very sexy; he just needed petty deception to make him feel young and independent.

"Maybe Lyle's just a little too perfect," I went on. "How can you feel good about the way you look standing next to a Ken doll? There's something sexy about a guy who—I don't know—doesn't seem *complete*."

"It's not sexy to be complete?" Stephen said. "Then there's hope for me yet."

"Don't say that," I said. "Nobody's more complete than

you." I knelt down and put my arm around his shoulders.

"I worry sometimes that the rest of my life will be ex-actly like this afternoon: just looking," Stephen said matter-of-factly. He hardly ever sounded self-pitying, despite the prognosis he might never move his left arm or walk without aid.

"I know what you mean," Veronica said quietly.

She looked sadder than I'd ever remembered seeing her. At once I felt a pang of guilt for having a life that made me seem at least reasonably happy in her eyes. I looked away from her and watched Stephen, who was studying another photo. He had a right to be sad, too, more than he let on. But I can't say that he was, at least not the way I saw it.

Maybe sadness, like beauty, is in the eye of the beholder.

"**H**ere's a good title," Veronica said. "How about *Somebody Up There Hates Me?*"

We pulled into the parking lot of the zoo. A soft wind had begun to blow, and the sky had grown overcast. Stephen hoisted himself from the car into the chair. The three of us passed right through the gates without so much as a look of disapproval from a zoo keeper who stood by the boarded-up ticket booth. One of the few advantages of having a wheel-chair was that people tended to both pity you and want to stay as far away from you as possible, a combination that allowed you to get away with a great many things.

"There is a chance you were wrong, don't you think?" Veronica asked as we made our way up a long hill. "The lighting in those bars must be so dark. It'd be easy to make a mistake."

"Veronica," I said. "Don't go down that road."

"What road?"

"That road where your mind gets all confused as to what's reality and what it is you want to believe no matter how much evidence is staring you right in the face."

"Peter, that's the street where I *live*," Veronica said.

Along the paths that led from cage to cage were trucks and trailers ready to haul away dilapidated zoo equipment along with a few animals that had yet to be moved out. We passed a habitat where a giraffe now stood alone in the mud.

We walked along a wire fence that surrounded a rocky area. At the top of the hill we found a bench where Veronica told Chad to meet her. I sat down while Veronica paced. Stephen moved his chair in front of the bench, facing me. When some branches stirred, Veronica darted her head, expecting to see Chad.

"Relax," I said to Veronica. "If you're patient, life eventually gets funnier. It never fails."

"I don't know about funnier," Stephen said. "But it sure can get more bearable, even if just for a little while. Thanks for taking me out today."

Veronica stood in back of Stephen and massaged his shoulders. "This feel OK?"

"Great," Stephen said. He closed his eyes.

A ram made its way from the top of the hill in the fenced area behind us. Its hooves clicked against the rocks.

Veronica spotted a pay phone a few feet away from the bench. "Shit. I never did check my messages for that job," she said. She was rubbing Stephen's shoulders faster and faster. "Look at me. I'm so tense."

"I bet if you call you'll find a message telling you to

come back for another interview. Or maybe they might even offer you the job," Stephen said.

"Or there might be a message from Chad telling me why he's late," Veronica said. "Do you think I should call, Peter?"

"How can you lose?" I said. It was easier for me to respond the way I thought Veronica wanted me to. "If they say yes, you've got your best friends to celebrate with. If they say no, you've got four loving shoulders to cry on."

"You think they're going to say no?" Veronica said.

"I didn't say that."

"But you implied it."

"You might feel better if you call, no matter what the news," Stephen said. "At least you'll know, right?"

Veronica made the call and returned to the bench a minute later.

"Well?" I said.

"I forgot my therapy appointment," she said. "They were calling to remind me. That was all. Can you believe it? I forgot to go to the Furniture Man so I could scream into a wing chair. Eighty bucks down the drain."

"It's still lunch hour," I said. "Maybe they'll call this afternoon."

"It's lunch hour in Bali," Veronica said. "Around here people finished eating hours ago." The ram brushed against the fence where Veronica was sitting. Veronica turned around and looked the ram in the eyes. "I feel like this guy, you know? Another single heterosexual roaming around with nothing to do."

Stephen rolled his chair closer to Veronica and took her hand. "It's hard to get a job in retail if you don't have any experience," he said. "Try not to be so disappointed. Maybe it's all a question of realistic expectations."

"Expectations?" Veronica said. "Christ, they can't get any lower. All I want is to be one of those people who *divides their time*. Like on the dust jackets of books where you read about a writer who *divides her time* between San Francisco and Boston. That's my problem. I don't even have anything to divide my time. Could somebody please tell me how my life got this way? I didn't even have a shitty childhood. It's so depressing."

When the rain started, the ram that was behind us made its way around the rock formations to find shelter. I looked at Stephen and realized this weather couldn't be healthy for him, and was about to say something when he spoke first.

"Is this him?" he said.

A dark-haired man carrying a bright yellow umbrella was walking our way from the bottom of the hill.

"Well, Peter?" Veronica said.

I squinted to see his face. "I'm afraid so."

"Fuck. Now what do I do?"

"We'll duck out," Stephen said suddenly. "Yell if you need us. Hop on, Peter." He spun his chair around, gripped the right wheel with his hand, and shoved himself off down the side of the hill opposite Chad.

I jumped on the foot stand in back of the wheelchair and soon we picked up speed. Stephen screamed like a little boy on a roller coaster. We finally slowed down at the edge of the lion's den where we came to a stop.

"Christ, Stephen," I said. I was laughing so hard I had to bend over to catch my breath. "Are you nuts?"

"That was great," Stephen said. His eyes were closed,

and he smiled as the rain hit his face.

"You're getting soaked," I said. "We've got to get you inside. They'll have my head if I bring you back to the hospital with a cold."

"Let's go in there." Stephen pointed towards the lion's exhibit.

A fence that had once surrounded the cement house had been knocked over, now waiting to be hauled away. The area was covered with dead grass, and the rain had made the animal smell in the exhibit even more pungent. I helped Stephen out of his chair and we both slid down the incline. I held him up as we walked to the house.

"You feeling all right?" I asked when we got inside.

"I'm fine," Stephen said. "Just a little tired."

I took off my shirt and pulled my T-shirt over my head. I didn't feel the least self-conscious; I knew Stephen wouldn't be sizing me up with photos he'd seen that morning of Lyle.

"Here," I said. I handed Stephen the T-shirt. "This isn't too wet. Dry your face off."

"Thanks," Stephen said. "I wish you didn't have to bring me back to the hospital today."

"You'll be out soon and I won't have to," I said. "It'll be wonderful, but I'll miss visiting you. I look forward to swinging by after work and sitting with you while you eat."

"Really?"

"It's the highlight of my day," I said. "It's important to me that you let me help you. You've spent your whole life giving and giving. I'm glad I can be there for you."

"I'm glad, too," Stephen said. "Knowing you're going to stick your head in the door is how I make it through the afternoon. God, I get so weary of Nurse Diesel. Does Theo ever mind you visiting as much as you do?"

"I don't think so. At least he doesn't say anything. These days we've been arguing a lot. Theo wants us to look into adopting a kid."

"Well?"

"I guess I just can't see Theo and me as fathers."

"I used to want kids," Stephen said. "I still do."

"You'd be a great father," I said. "You're the kindest person I know. And handsome, too."

"Thanks. You're very good to me."

I kissed him gently on the forehead. I wanted to tell him I loved him right then, to let him know that even though I did love Theo I didn't hand all my love over to him when we married, like signing over all my assets in bankruptcy court. I had told Stephen I loved him once before, long before I met Theo. He was flattered and sweet and told me he loved me, too, but his tone was lighter than mine. As he spoke, he touched me on the shoulder like an older brother, the way I might touch Veronica if I told her I loved her. I never broached the subject again.

I didn't say anything now, either. A silence had begun to settle between us when I heard Veronica call my name. I touched Stephen's knee as I stood to go out of the den to get her.

"Come join us," I said.

Veronica fell back against the wall and slid to the floor. She covered her face with her hands.

"I give up," she said.

"That bad?" I said.

"You were right, Peter," she said. "It was him. He apologized a thousand times, the bastard. Why couldn't he just lie or not show up so I could be completely furious with him?"

"What did he say?" Stephen asked.

"He said that he thought there was a little spark between us so he decided to go with it, but that in the end he just can't be someone he's not."

"Better to find out now," I said. "You don't know how many gay men I know who are in straight marriages."

"Then he looks at me and says, 'You know, Veronica, there's much to admire in you. I'm sorry it didn't work out.' *Much to admire.* Shit, it sounds like another one of our titles, Peter. *Much to Admire, Little to Love.*"

I put my arm around her. She dropped her head on my shoulder. I could feel her sopping wet hair on my chest. Across from me, Stephen was massaging his hand, working it as if he were kneading dough. The doctors had told him to do this periodically to keep the hand from atrophying. If he got some more feeling back, they wanted to be sure the muscles still worked.

"What does it matter?" Veronica said with a laugh. "We all know that you're the one I love, Peter. All the other guys in my life are just distractions."

"I'm sorry," I said.

Veronica looked around the lion's shelter. "I used to love this zoo. It always made me happy, no matter what was going on in my life. I could always feel like a child again. Now there's nothing left of it."

"I read the other day that some zoo's going to have a human exhibit," Stephen said. "It's sort of like us in this house. It's going to be a couple. Straight, of course. Man and a woman."